# HyperLinkz

# Spam Alert

## BOOK 4 ROBERT ELMER

WaterBrook
PRESS

SPAM ALERT
PUBLISHED BY WATERBROOK PRESS
2375 Telstar Drive, Suite 160
Colorado Springs, Colorado 80920
*A division of Random House, Inc.*

All Scripture quotations, unless otherwise indicated, are taken from the *Holy Bible, New International Version*®. NIV®. Copyright © 1973, 1978, 1984 by International Bible Society. Used by permission of Zondervan Publishing House. All rights reserved.

Unless noted in "The Hyperlinkz Guide to Safe Surfing," all Web-site names are fabrications of the author.

ISBN 1-57856-750-5

Library of Congress Cataloging-in-Publication Data has been requested.

Printed in the United States of America
2004—First Edition

10 9 8 7 6 5 4 3 2 1

# Contents

# Introducing...Spam ALert

Austin T. Webster here. Even though I live in a town called Normal, hardly anything seems that way since my sister, Ashley, and I were accidentally sucked into the Internet.

If you don't believe me, I don't blame you; I know it sounds totally wacko. I wouldn't have believed it myself if I hadn't been there, riding a search engine, walking through Web sites, and talking to digital people as though they were part of the real world.

If you've read our first three adventures, *Digital Disaster,* *Fudge Factor,* and *Web Jam,* you know just what I'm talking about. And you might be wondering if Ashley, Jessi, and the other girls from Chiddix Junior High got home after being trapped online at the end of *Web Jam.* Well, I took care of that. Okay, so it took a little longer than I thought—about ten tries, with e-mails and attachments routed through my computer. But in the end I finally brought them all back to Normal again, no problem.

There is still one big problem though—Mattie Blankenskrean, the head of the NCCC, which stands for the Normal Council on Civil Correctness. The thing is, *she* decides what's correct or not. For instance, Mattie's not too happy about Jesus or Bible miracles or anything about faith being on the Internet. When Ashley and I met her, she was trying to erase anything like that clean off the Web. Maybe she thought that if it wasn't there, not as many people would believe it.

Good thing Mattie's disappeared for a while. Since school has started up again, all we have to worry about are taking math tests and writing papers.

Oh—and a tornado.

# CHAPTER 1

# Twister Busters

"YEE-haw!" Austin's friend Drew Scarola gripped the steering wheel of their hopped-up four-wheel-drive SUV as they bounced down a gravel road in the middle of nowhere.

It was a good thing they were in the middle of nowhere since, like Austin, Drew still had about three years to go before he'd be old enough for an Illinois State driver's license. And Drew could have used another couple inches of leg to reach the gas pedal and brake without slouching in the driver's seat.

*Slam!* They hit another pothole head-on. Austin held on, his eyes following the twister on the very cool Doppler radar screen beside him.

The SUV had every electronic gizmo you could imagine—and a whole lot more you probably couldn't. A satellite navigation system to tell them exactly where they were. Wind-speed indicators. Temperature sensors. Barometers. And a whole collection of computer monitors, each one flashing a different kind of readout.

"Here comes another bump!" screeched Drew, and Austin braced against the dashboard in front of him with both hands. It didn't do any good. *Whump!*

"Aw, man." Austin grinned as he rubbed his head. "You almost put me through the roof that time."

"I think we're catching up to it." Drew didn't seem to be paying much attention to the bumps and gullies they flew over on the country road. Or to the sea of waving corn that stretched in all directions. Not with the ink-black storm clouds up ahead—and the wicked-looking funnel cloud that dipped to touch the ground, daring them to come closer.

The tornado.

Austin tried to scribble down what he saw, at least as much as he could between the bumps. Stuff like: *old red barn explodes in2 million toothpicks, picked up in2 cloud.* He figured that kind of thing would sound pretty good later if he had to write up a science report. Or *golf ball–size hail pounds hood of Suburban.* He tried to see through the downpour that was so heavy it reminded him of the banana shake he'd made himself in the blender last Sunday after church.

Tree branches and fence posts flew at them like missiles looking for a mark. A hunk of twisted green metal—maybe from a tractor—hit the road just ahead of them. Could be this trip wasn't such a good idea after all.

"Slow down!" Austin yelled, his voice already hoarse from shouting.

*Thunk!* A chunk of wood slammed against the roof of the SUV, and Drew swerved to keep from hitting something else. The poor guy could hardly see over the steering wheel, but he was doing the best he could.

All of a sudden, though, he and Austin had something much bigger to worry about. As Drew slammed on the brakes, they could see the sky darkening, its shadow growing. Even with the wind blasting and the hail clunking against the SUV, they could hear the sound of a hundred freight trains coming straight at them.

Drew's face turned white.

"Uh, Austin? Think maybe we've seen enough?"

Austin nodded. He quickly rolled down his window and squinted out to the side to read the links written in big letters across the cornfields, but hail pelted him on the side of the head.

"Where are the links?" Drew shouted.

Drew meant the parts of the Web site they could press or step on to go to another place on the Internet. Just now anyplace else seemed like a great idea.

"I'm not sure." Austin held up his hand against the hail. "But put it in reverse!"

"Huh?" Drew acted as if he'd never heard of going backward. Okay, so he hadn't taken driver's ed yet, but it didn't take a genius to figure out that anything was better than forward.

*Crash!* A broken piece of two-by-four skewered the side of the SUV, sending a shower of sparks out one of the computer screens.

*Whoops.*

"Reverse!" Austin yelled with his last bit of voice. He reached over to the gearshift and shoved it into the *R* position. "Hit it!"

Drew may not have known how to drive very well yet, but he'd said he knew how to handle his Uncle Jerry's John Deere tractor. And he sure knew how to "hit it." Austin nearly got whiplash as they peeled out of their spot on the gravel road, and the front end of the SUV started to shake and bounce up and down in the wild wind.

They crashed through the corn just ahead of the twister. It was stripping the dry stalks like one of those triple-action shavers Austin always saw on the TV commercials.

"Faster!" he whimpered. Even if this was only a Web site, he didn't want to get sucked up into a tornado. He glanced over his shoulder for a link. Anything would do right now.

They blew by *Weather Service Info* and then *The Science of*

*Tornadoes.* Those would have been fine, but at least he could see other sites, too. Drew was obviously doing his best to steer straight backward.

Then Austin saw it.

"Stop!" He grabbed Drew's shoulder and pointed at the *Contact Us* e-mail link. As they screeched to a stop, he threw open the door, which flew off its hinges and bounced off through the cornfield. They would have one chance to step into their escape link, the one that would e-mail them back to Austin's laptop.

Only one shot.

# CHAPTER 2

# Storm Warning

Ashley Webster pulled up the hood of her orange rain poncho and walked a little faster down Oak Street and around the corner toward school. Chiddix Junior High wasn't too far from their home on Fell Avenue. Of course, their home wasn't too far from anywhere in Normal, Illinois, since Normal wasn't that big of a town—unless you were walking in the pouring rain. Like Ashley was now.

"Slow down, Ash." Her Aunt Jessica did her best to keep up, but as usual Ashley was in the lead.

And even though Jessi was Ashley's aunt, they both went to Chiddix. Weird but true, *Aunt* Jessica was the way youngest sister of Ashley's mom and only a few months apart in age from Ashley herself. Sometimes it happens that way—just not very often.

"Sorry." Ashley hadn't meant to leave her friend behind. She hopped a puddle, doing a half-spin in midair, while Jessi caught up. "I'm just thinking about what's going on with Austin."

"You mean you're wondering why he's not walking with us this morning?" Jessi clearly didn't have a clue what Ashley meant, but then, did she ever?

"I mean why he left a half-hour early. He's up to something, and I don't think it's homework."

"Maybe he's meeting a girl." Jessi giggled at the idea.

"Yeah, right. And maybe our soccer team is going to win the state finals this year."

"Oh, come on. You're not *that* bad. If everybody else was as good as you, you'd win, no problem. In fact…"

Jessi went on as Ashley again puzzled over what her brother was up to. His science project maybe? They still had two weeks before it was due. That meant Austin wouldn't be starting on it for another week and six days. Practicing for the Knowledge Bowl? Maybe, but the library wasn't usually open this early. No, she decided, Austin was up to something unusual, and it was up to her to find out what.

The rain poured down harder, and she wished they'd brought their umbrellas. Oh well. A minivan pulled up next to them, and a window rolled down.

"You guys want a ride?" It was Nattie, a girl on Ashley's soccer team.

"Sure!" Jessi piped up.

"No thanks." Ashley held back. "We're almost there. We need the exercise."

"Oh." Nattie looked at them and shrugged. "We were just listening to the tornado-watch reports when we saw you. Guess I'll see you at school then."

As Nattie's window zipped back up, Ashley looked at the black skies. She'd lived here in Tornado Alley all her life, but she'd never seen a real tornado up close and in person before. She hoped today wouldn't change that.

"Oh, wow!" Austin stared at the ceiling light in one of the school's piano practice rooms. Chiddix Junior High had a half-dozen rooms like this, little rooms with just enough space for a piano and a bench and floor-to-ceiling bumpy foam to keep in the sound. Best of all, the doors locked—and Austin had a key.

"That was amazing." Drew picked himself up off the carpeted floor. His wet, black hair was matted to his forehead, and his clothes looked as if he'd fallen into a swimming pool. Next to them, up on the piano, Austin's trusty, silver laptop purred and sputtered as it returned to normal, as Drew and Austin had just done.

"Crazy," agreed Austin, getting to his feet.

"Absolutely nuts."

"Insane."

"Wigged out."

They looked at each other and grinned.

"So when are we going in again?" Drew may have been one of the shortest guys in the school, but he had guts. He always told everyone it was because of his Italian grandfather.

Austin laughed at his friend. He'd felt the exact same way the first time he and his sister, Ashley, had been inside the Internet. He'd hated it. He'd loved it. He'd been scared out of his wits. He couldn't wait to go again.

Speaking of Ashley, Austin guessed she wasn't going to be too happy about his taking somebody else into the Web to show him around. She'd say it was too dangerous. But he'd have to deal with that later.

*Knock, knock, knock.* Drew pointed to the view window in the practice-room door behind them.

Austin turned to see the face of Mr. Witherwax, the school's head janitor. (People called him Mr. Dub for short.) Some kids said he was good buddies with Mr. Chiddix himself, but the original John C. Chiddix had retired way back in 1960, so Austin wasn't sure whether that was true. For sure Mr. Dub was pretty old though. And he had a good set of knuckles for rapping on the head-size window.

"What are you boys doing here so early?" he asked as Austin cracked open the door.

Early as in twenty minutes before classes began.

None of his possible answers would have sounded right, thought Austin, especially not the true ones. But he didn't need to worry about coming up with one. Mr. Dub didn't give him a chance.

"Well, get on out of here and dry off while you're at it. I knew it was raining outside, but you boys…"

Austin didn't wait for the rest of the lecture. Knowing Drew still had the digital camera, Austin grabbed his laptop and sprinted down the hall toward their lockers.

# CHAPTER 3

# Mr. Z

At least Austin and Drew weren't the only ones who were dripping wet in class that morning. When Nick Ortiz sloshed through the door of Mrs. Sanders's classroom, he looked as if he'd been swimming in the same pool.

"Haven't any of you boys heard of raincoats?" Tucker Campbell shrugged out of her burgundy red, oh-so-coordinated all-weather coat, which she'd no doubt picked up the last time her mom took her shopping at the ultrafancy Marshall Field's department store in Chicago.

Austin flashed back his best you-don't-bother-me-at-all smile and made his way past Laurie Parker and Brian McGonigle, who were talking about—what else?—the tornadoes yesterday and the tornado watch today.

"Your sister was looking for you," Tucker told Austin just as he tuned in to the tornado talk.

Laurie was saying she had a cousin who lived in Stanford,

only a few miles away, and somebody had seen a funnel cloud there yesterday, though it hadn't touched down.

"I *said*..." Tucker tried again.

"I'll catch up to her between classes." Austin had to be polite. "Thanks."

Brian topped Laurie by saying he'd seen a tornado pretty close up when he was eight. Drew started to ask how close when a substitute teacher walked in.

Austin didn't have anything against sandals; a guy could wear them if he wanted to. And tie-dye shirts were sort of groovy, if you liked that sixties style. Even beards were okay. In fact, Austin supposed a teacher could wear anything he liked. But he heard Tucker Campbell catch her breath as in "uh-oh."

"Hey, guys." Their substitute nodded hello to them and dumped a pile of books on the teacher's desk. "I'm here for Mrs. Sanders's language arts classes today."

Then he did what every substitute teacher always did: He wrote his name in big, careful letters at the top of the whiteboard, only he used three different color markers.

RAVEN ZAWISTOKOWSKI.

The last four letters looked sort of squished together since they ran to the end of the board.

Somebody snickered in the back row, probably Nick. Snickering was what he did best.

"What kind of a name is Raven Zimmer...whatever?" he whispered too loudly.

"What kind of a name is Raven Zawistokowski?" The sub laughed, and it sounded as if he'd heard that question plenty of times before.

A couple of girls glared at Nick for being rude, but that was just Nick, and he shrugged.

"It's the name my parents gave me," the sub went on, "when they lived on a commune in upstate New York. Sure, most people think it's a little unusual, but I never get confused with anyone else. You can call me Raven or Mr. Z. It's all good."

A hand went up—Laurie Parker in the front row. No surprise there. Laurie would be the first one to ask a question, guaranteed.

"Er...Mr. Z, are we going to be able to listen to the radio for tornado warnings today?"

"That's a good thought..."—he held up one hand as he searched his seating chart for her name—"Laurie. I appreciate your bringing that up, since we had some tornado sightings yesterday and—"

"GOOD MORNING, CHIDDIX CHARGERS!" Mr. Hayward's voice came booming over the classroom loudspeaker the way it did every morning at exactly 8:12. Along with the regular announcements, he reminded students that they needed to turn in their yearbook orders, that the chess club was meeting during lunch, and that girls' soccer practice was going to be in the gym due to the weather, unless it was canceled.

"And speaking of the weather," he added. "I'm sure all of you are aware of the tornado watch that's in effect. Remember, that doesn't necessarily mean there is going to be a tornado, only that conditions are right for one. Your teachers know what to do in case the tornado *watch* turns into a tornado *warning*. In other words, if an actual tornado is sighted, just do as they direct. I don't want any of you to worry."

Too late. Laurie Parker had already started hyperventilating, breathing faster than a scared rabbit.

Mr. Z looked up at the speaker in the wall. "Sounds like that's it. Time to get to work."

Tornado or no tornado, the day would go on as normal at Chiddix Junior High School. They plowed through the daily assignment sheets, counted how many were going to have lunch that day, and finally got to their English assignment. That's when Mr. Z dropped the bomb.

# CHAPTER 4

# Easy A

"Ten pages, single-spaced, due in two weeks," Mr. Z explained as he handed out the assignment sheet. Everyone's jaws hit the floor, including Austin's. "You can choose to write about anyone from the list I'm going to write on the board."

Okay, so Mrs. Sanders had warned them they'd have to write a biography. But *ten* pages? Wasn't that almost as long as *War and Peace,* a humungous book Austin had once seen on the library shelf?

All right, maybe ten pages wasn't quite *that* long. But even to Austin, who was sort-of the star of the Chiddix Junior High Knowledge Bowl team, ten pages seemed like a death sentence. At least they could do the reports with a partner, which was good.

"I'm going to add a little spice to your teacher's assignment." Mr. Z smiled as if he was having a great old time. "I'd like you to choose a famous *thinking* writer to report on.

When Mrs. Sanders comes back tomorrow, you're going to blow her away with the interesting people you've chosen."

"Some of those guys didn't think?" asked Nick, waving his sheet. "Cool."

That brought a laugh from the rest of the class. Of course, Nick could read the phone book aloud, and somebody would giggle. That was just Nick.

"You're laughing. But you'd be surprised at the amount of mindless material out there. Just because it's in print doesn't mean it's worth reading."

Austin had heard that someplace before. Maybe from his dad. *Hmmm, could be this sub isn't so bad after all.*

Of course, the question now was which author they would choose to write about, which sent Mr. Z trotting to the board.

"I'm going to write here the names of ten famous writers *I* suggest."

"Does Mrs. Sanders know about this?" asked Laurie, but Mr. Z ignored the question as he started writing.

"This writer's one of my favorites." Mr. Z pointed to a name he'd just written. "He wrote, 'Everyone knows how to find the meaning of life within themselves.' Recognize that line?"

Everyone in the class gave him blank stares. Even Nick didn't have a funny comeback for that one. Mr. Z's list was starting to look pretty weird, not to mention his quote. While everybody sank lower and lower in their seats, Mr. Z went on to list more names even Austin had never heard of before.

"Who *are* these people?" whispered Drew.

This time it was Austin's turn to raise his hand.

"Mr. Z, can we do a famous thinking author not on your list?"

The substitute finished writing name number ten on his list, a guy named Aldous Huxley. "That depends on whom you had in mind, Mr. Webster."

Now *that* was weird, but Austin wasn't sure if anybody else noticed. Not that the sub called him Mr. Webster, but that he knew Austin's voice and name without even turning around or looking at the seating chart.

But Austin wasn't going to let that stop him.

"I was thinking Drew and I could do a report on a British author who died on the same day as Huxley—and John F. Kennedy, too."

"And that would be when?" Mr. Z was still facing the whiteboard.

"Uh…" Austin knew the answer. But as usual it took a second or two to travel from his brain to his mouth. "November 22, 1963."

Finally their substitute turned around and stared straight at Austin.

"How did you know that?"

"He's on the Chiddix Knowledge Bowl team." Drew put in a good word for his friend. "He knows all kinds of trivia like that. It just comes out of his head...well, eventually it does."

A few kids giggled, which helped lighten things up.

"Far out." Mr. Z smiled as he put down his marker. "But if you're thinking of C. S. Lewis, I'm not sure it would be appropriate to write about him. He was a religious author."

*More like a* Christian *author.* Austin wondered how Mr. Z had guessed who he was going to suggest. Maybe he was good at trivia too. Or maybe not.

"After all," the sub went on, "our Constitution says we should have a separation of church and state."

Austin knew that wasn't exactly true. And he didn't want to sound snotty or like a know-it-all, but...

"Excuse me, sir," he asked, "but doesn't it just say we can't have a state religion that everybody has to join, the way some countries do?"

Mr. Z frowned. "It's hardly that simple, and this is really a discussion for social studies."

But Austin wasn't ready to give up.

"C. S. Lewis wrote some science fiction, too. Plus some kids books and a lot of other stuff. Drew and I just thought—"

"Yes, I'm sure you did. And would you and Drew be planning to conduct your research on the Internet this time?"

*This time?* Okay, this was getting downright creepy. What did Mr. Z know, and how did he know it? Even Drew looked over at Austin with a question on his face.

Their substitute couldn't know about their hyperlink adventures, could he?

"Well," Austin managed, "maybe we'll do a little online research, but—"

"All right, then." Mr. Z didn't let him finish. "As long as the report doesn't turn into a sermon."

*Whoa. Where did that come from?*

But Mr. Z moved on. "And I'd like to have you two work with someone who doesn't have a partner yet." He glanced down the row. "Nick, you can develop some cooperative learning strategies with these two gentlemen. Pull up your chair."

"Cool." Nick grinned as he slowly moved up to join them. "Whatever that is."

"But…" Austin's mouth flapped open. Nick, who had flunked fourth grade. Nick, who had cheated on every test he'd ever taken. Nick, who had eaten a live goldfish the first day of school just to gross everyone out.

And now Nick was working with him and Drew? The kid who had been secretly voted Most Likely to End Up in Prison hiked up his sagging pants, sat down backward in his chair, and held up his hand for a high-five.

"Easy A, huh?" he asked them.

"Yeah." Austin returned the high-five, then rubbed his forehead where a headache was starting. "Easy A."

It looked to him as if Mr. Z was smiling.

# CHAPTER 5

# Dot Con Artist

"Give it a break, Austin," Drew whispered to him as they packed up to leave first period. "He's strange, but you don't think he's a criminal, do you?"

*Maybe.* But Austin knew the school wouldn't let anyone teach unless that person was a real teacher and had fingerprints on file and FBI checks and all that. So Mr. Z had to have a clean record, right?

"Meet you after lunch for study hall in the library, huh?" Nick asked as he pushed his chair back to his desk. "I haven't been in the library much. They have any skater magazines, you think?"

Austin groaned. He could see it now. He and Drew would do all the work while Nick goofed off. But he couldn't worry about it now. Something else was bothering him more.

"How do you think Mr. Z knew my name?" he wondered aloud to Drew.

"Maybe he's seen you before," Drew shrugged. "Or maybe he knows your dad from the hospital. Why don't you ask him?"

"Are you kidding? Then he'll *know* I know." Austin glanced at Mr. Z, who looked as if he was answering yet another of Laurie's questions before she left the room.

Drew stood on a chair to put a writing textbook back up on the shelf.

"*What* do you know, Austin?"

"That's just it. I don't know anything. But what about that weird question about us on the Internet?"

"Yeah," Drew finally agreed as he stepped down. "I've gotta admit that was a little strange. Maybe he just said that for no reason."

"No way. I'm telling you, Drew, he knows. I don't know how he knows, but he knows."

"Hmm."

"So listen. I need you to do something."

Drew looked unsure at first, but he actually did a pretty good acting job when the class filed out into the hall. If Austin hadn't known better, he'd have thought Drew really *was* choking to death right outside the classroom door.

"You okay?" Mr. Z rushed to see if Drew was all right while Austin slipped into one of the coat closets.

*This had better be worth it,* he thought, balancing himself on top of a stack of dusty textbooks. He tried not to breathe too much of the musty air.

"Crazy kids," mumbled Mr. Z, closing the door with a click and jangling his key chain. It sounded to Austin as if the substitute had also closed and latched the outside windows, which were barely open anyway.

What was going on out there? Austin pressed his ear to the closet-door vent so he wouldn't miss a thing. He dared a peek and saw the sub open the classroom door to check the hallway and then close it carefully before he pulled a cell phone from his backpack and punched in a number.

Mr. Z jumped right in. "I haven't seen it yet."

No "Hello, this is Raven." Just "I haven't seen it yet." Austin would have given anything to hear the other side of that phone chat.

"I know…but what do you expect me to do, Mattie? Just break into the guy's locker?"

*Mattie? As in Mattie Blankenskrean, head of the NCCC?* The Websters hadn't seen her in weeks, not since she had tried to bleach every shred of faith from the Web—with Austin and his sister still inside it. Now *there* was a crazy woman. And whose locker were they talking about?

Austin was afraid he knew.

"Listen, I'll get the camera, all right? But I have another class in a few minutes and then a free period before lunch."

He paused before cutting right back in.

"Yes, I know it's not the only way inside the Web. But do *they* know?"

Another pause.

"Okay, then I have an idea. If I can locate the computer, I'll erase the hard drive. That should keep them out for at least a little while. And no one will ever suspect."

Taking his camera? Erasing his laptop? What more did Austin need to know?

Mr. Z suddenly hung up without a good-bye.

Drew was pounding on a window, waving for the teacher to open up.

*He's nuts,* thought Austin, *but he's beautiful.*

Austin knew he couldn't sit in the closet any longer, especially not after what he'd just heard. Besides, his foot had nearly fallen asleep, and the dust was triggering his allergies. *Should I try to leave now?* He cracked open the door as Mr. Z went to open the window.

"Hey!" yelled Drew. "I need to ask you something really important."

The closet door squeaked a little, and Austin froze—but only for a second. He knew he had about five seconds to tip-toe across the room behind Mr. Z's back. Drew was going on and on about funnel clouds and tornadoes, wondering if Mr. Z had seen one out that direction. He pointed.

Austin took one more step to the door, turned the knob oh so quietly, and slipped out.

"I can't believe it." Once he was out in the hallway and around the corner from the room, he finally let himself take a deep breath.

But what now? He checked up and down the halls to make sure Mr. Z hadn't followed him. Then he stopped in front of his locker and snapped open the heavy-duty combination lock. He'd have to hurry or he'd be late to his next class. After punching in the security code on his locker alarm, Austin grabbed the green backpack with his laptop inside and reset the alarm.

Just to be sure.

# CHAPTER 6

# Locker ALarm

Austin had almost made it to the lunchroom later that day when he heard his name over the school loudspeakers.

"Austin Webster to the counseling center immediately, please. Austin Webster."

What now? He detoured back to the office, where one of the secretaries pointed him toward the assistant principal's office, which doubled as the counseling center.

"Come on in, Austin. Have a seat." Mr. Metzger was a nice and comfy kind of guy, no doubt about it. He wore nice and comfy tan slacks and a nice and comfy denim shirt and leaned back in his nice and comfy leather easy chair.

Everything else in the office seemed nice and comfy too. The shelf full of friendly looking books and a poster of a kitten. The blue Cubs batting helmet on the wall. Just the sort of place you'd want to curl up and take a nap. Only Austin was pretty sure that wasn't why he'd been called here.

Just outside the door Austin could hear the drone of the tornado news. People in the office had been listening to it all day.

"Am I in trouble?" Austin asked to make sure.

Mr. Metzger laughed, "You tell me." The school counselor, who lately had been filling in as assistant principal, leaned forward in his chair to face Austin. "Are you?"

"Well, I was just wondering because you called me here."

"It sounds like you're a little unsettled about being called to my office. Is that fair to say?"

"Sure, Mr. Metzger. But what did you want to see me about?"

Mr. Metzger pressed the tips of his fingers into the shape of a tent and took a deep breath as if what he was going to say was very important.

"That's a good question, Austin. You see, I received a call this morning about a certain piece of equipment you're known to have here on campus." The counselor paused. "Actually, two pieces of equipment, both of which, according to Chiddix General Handbook, page seven, paragraph two, are forbidden on school grounds."

*Uh-oh.* Austin had a pretty good idea who had made the call and why. He planted his feet solidly in front of his backpack just in case Mr. Metzger was going to make a grab for it. Mr. Z sure was trying everything to grab Austin's equipment and keep him off the Internet.

"You're not talking about my laptop and digital camera, are you?" he asked.

"I'm glad we're coming to an understanding about this," the counselor smiled. "I was afraid confiscating your items would be...well, awkward. But I'm sure you know why students can't be allowed to bring those kinds of things to school."

"Sure, sir, I understand. But I have special permission from Miss Myers to bring my stuff when we're working on the yearbook." Miss Myers was the yearbook advisor. "My parents even signed a permission slip she gave them."

Mr. Metzger coughed and grabbed his phone.

"Judy, what's the scoop on the Webster kid's bringing his laptop and... Oh. Why didn't you tell me about this before?" He listened for a moment, his cheeks blazing cherry red. "No, of course not. No problem here. In fact, we were having a wonderful chat."

Taking that as his signal to leave, Austin stood up.

But Mr. Metzger held up his hand for him to stay.

"Well, that clears things up, doesn't it?" The man smiled as if nothing had happened. "I'm glad we dialogued."

*Dialogued?*

"Okay, sir. Is that all?"

"Actually, there is one more thing. I've been hearing rumors, and it's my job to check them out, no matter how odd."

"Odd?" Austin backed up to the door. He wasn't going to miss any more of lunch period than he had to.

"I want you to know that I understand how Internet games can seem as if they're real. Have you ever noticed that?"

*Good grief!* What had Mr. Z been telling him?

"Not exactly. I'm not very good at those games. Drew always beats me."

"I see. You're saying that Drew Scarola plays these games with you? How much time would you say the two of you spend at these games?"

"Not very much. A few minutes, once in a while."

"And would you say that when you're playing these computer games, you feel as if you're really there?"

Oh, brother. He *had* been talking to Mr. Z. Only he couldn't know the whole story, or he wouldn't be asking all these counselor questions.

"Naw, most computer games are lame. Sometimes I'd rather read a book."

Mr. Metzger brightened right up, the way Austin knew he would.

"There you go!" The counselor slapped him on the back. "You just keep right on doing that. Have a good lunch."

Austin made his escape at last, but not before he looked over his shoulder to see Mr. Metzger writing something in a folder. Probably something like, *Case Study 101: Austin T.*

*Webster, grade 7. Prognosis: overactive imagination. Reportedly thinks video games are real, despite his claims that he would rather read. Follow up in four weeks to monitor progress.*

Oh well. Mr. Metzger could think whatever he wanted. Austin didn't have time to worry about it.

He was headed toward the cafeteria when a strange sound made him stop.

*Whoop, whoop, whoop!*

It couldn't be.

But when Drew came sprinting down the hall, Austin knew it was. His friend slid to a stop. "Your locker alarm, Austin!"

*Whoop, whoop...*

"Somebody's been in your locker!"

# CHAPTER 7

# Web and Go Seek

"I knew Nick wasn't going to show." Drew leaned back in his chair and rubbed his forehead as their after-lunch study hall ticked away. "He probably had to go steal some candy from the student store first."

"That's a little harsh, don't you think?" Austin set another encyclopedia on the library worktable—volume *L* for Lewis, C. S.

"I guess so." Drew shrugged. "But—"

"He was the one who told us about Mr. Z messing with my locker, right?"

"Yeah, if you can believe him. I mean, even if he says he thinks he saw Mr. Z coming down the hall right after the alarm went off… Well, you never know."

"What if he's right though? And look, the office has the combinations to everyone's lockers, mine included. We could find out if Mr. Z checked my file for the combo."

"Right. Maybe you could just ask him straight up, like 'Hey, Mr. Z, did you find what you were looking for?'"

Austin sighed. He had only known Drew since this past summer, a few months ago. But it was long enough to know that his friend was probably right.

"Hey, guys." The door to the library banged open, hitting the inside wall. Nick was good at grand entrances. "Haven't seen you since the cafeteria line. Did you miss me?"

Good thing Mrs. Peterson, the librarian, was off shelving books at the far side of the library. Even so, she gave them a warning look.

Nick didn't exactly look prepared to study. He was dragging a half-full, oversize black garbage bag behind him. What was he doing?

"Forgot to tell you I'm on detention today during lunch and after school. Garbage detail for Mr. Hayward."

"Oh." Austin watched him dump the paper from a small wastebasket into the bag. "Looks fun, but lunch is over."

"Yeah, I know. Just have a couple more to finish up here. Wanna help?"

"Uh…"

"Kidding." Nick held up his hand. "You two brains just write me up a good report so I can look good reading it. Who's it supposed to be on again?"

"C. S. Lewis." Drew held up the encyclopedia that showed a picture of the British writer. "He wrote—"

"That's okay," Nick interrupted. "You can save it for your pal Mr. Z. He was pretty excited about us writing about this guy, right?"

They all chuckled—maybe the first time they had laughed *with* Nick rather than at him.

"Besides," he added, "he was coming down the hall right behind me a couple of minutes ago. I think he wants to talk to you guys."

"What?" Austin nearly fell off his chair. "He's coming this way?"

"Testing, one, two, three." Nick leaned over and rapped on the top of Austin's head. "I think that's what I said. Isn't that what I said, Drew?"

"Never mind." Austin jumped up from the table and grabbed his backpack. He pointed at Drew. "Got the camera?"

Drew nodded as they flew toward the door.

"Hey, wait a minute, you guys." Nick followed with his trash bag. "Are you really that scared of this guy?"

"Not scared." Austin knelt down and peeked out through the door at floor level—just in time to see Mr. Z walk out of the men's room and start back down the hall toward the library. "We just don't want to see him right now."

"Why not? Why's he after you? And why was he digging in your locker anyway?"

"No time to explain." Austin headed for the side door. "If he asks, don't tell him where we're headed."

"Where's that?"

"Music practice—I mean, never mind."

"Okay, I'll block him with the trash." Nick grabbed his trash bag as Mrs. Peterson came to see what was going on. Austin and Drew started to slip out the other door as Mr. Z walked in.

"Hey, boys, wait a minute!" Mr. Z stepped over the trash bag Nick had tossed his way. "I want to talk to you about your paper."

*Sure, you do.* Austin wasn't getting within ten feet of the guy, or he'd probably grab his laptop and erase his hard drive.

"Go!" He and Drew sprinted down the back hallway around the cafeteria. "To the practice rooms!"

Austin almost fell on his face as they skidded into the dead-end hallway with the practice rooms on each side. He pushed into the last room on the right.

*SLAM!* Drew locked the door, and they both knelt in the dark, trying to catch their breath.

"Is he still after us?" Drew asked.

Austin wasn't sure what might happen if Mr. Z *was* after

them. What would Austin say to Principal Hayward? "He stole my camera and erased my hard drive, sir. So now I can't travel online anymore."

Yeah, right.

"Someone's coming!" Drew hissed a warning.

A light went on in the outside hall.

"Quick," said Austin. "Set up the camera and hit the timer."

"You mean we're going in again? Now?"

"Just for a couple of minutes."

"But what about your laptop?"

Austin peeked out of the room before he opened his computer and brought up a Web site—a nice, safe one on C. S. Lewis—and adjusted a couple of settings.

"I have it programmed now so we come straight home through this link after we find what we need, and as long as the laptop stays on, the link will stay open. It'll be quicker if we don't have to go through e-mail."

"Great, but I mean, is your laptop safe here? You sure nobody'll find it?"

"Well, I hate to leave it here"—Austin tucked the laptop into the middle of a pile of coats in a box labeled "Chiddix PTA Coat Drive"—"but the door's locked and we'll be gone, so Mr. Z won't know we were ever here. It's got to be safer stashed here than in my locker."

Or at least Austin hoped it would be. He'd taken the laptop with him before, but the direct link would work really slick.

"And this way," he went on, "all we need to bring is the camera, since we can't leave it just sitting out in the open."

Now he could hear someone rattling doorknobs down at the other end of the hall, coming their way.

Quick! The leash to the camera? Ready? Timer set? Yes!

Austin and Drew stood up against the wall as the flash went off.

# CHAPTER 8

# FLash Spam

"Hey, Austin, this is pretty nice." Drew looked up the narrow, old cobblestone street where they'd landed. Brick and brownstone two-story buildings leaned in on them, giving the place an old English feel. "Sort of seems like somewhere you'd find a fairy-tale castle, huh?"

"I think it's supposed to be Oxford University," explained Austin, as a clock tower chimed.

"Cool. But do you think we'll be back in time for class?"

"Not a problem. All we need to do is meet Professor Lewis, find out about the man's books, take a couple of snapshots, and we'll probably be back before study hall is even over. Hopefully Mr. Z will have given up looking for us by then."

"Are you kidding?" Drew looked at his watch.

"Well, it's kind of hard to figure. Time here doesn't always work the way you expect; it goes much faster than back home in Normal. That's why it might seem to us like we've been gone for hours, but when we get back, only a few minutes will have gone by."

"Oh. Like in Mr. Lewis's Narnia books."

"Yeah, like that. Now all we have to do is find him."

Austin looked up and down the street, wondering where to find an Oxford professor. *Probably in an Oxford classroom,* he thought as he peeked in a shop window.

"And now for the latest spam report on *www-dot-YourWebWeather-dot-com.*" A smiling, puppet-size weatherman popped up in the reflection as if the window were a TV screen. He pointed behind him at a map, only Austin couldn't quite make out what was on it.

"What's this?" Drew asked. "The weather news? Here?"

"Today we're expecting three to six inches of serious junk e-mail sweeping through a number of history Web sites," the guy told them, still flashing his pearly whites in a huge smile. "With a special flash-flood alert for Web sites that have a lot of words or sites about writers. This is Chad Spaminelli," he said, "and I'm outta here, but thanks for watching."

Austin and Drew looked at each other.

"Didn't you say this was a C. S. Lewis site?" Drew asked.

Austin thought it was. So what was up with the sudden sound of white-water rapids? Not to mention the knee-deep wall of tumbling, jellylike junk bearing down on them from several blocks down the cobblestone lane. The strange flash flood, if that's what it was, was taking out shop signs and bi-cycles and sending people running.

"Yikes!" Drew turned to run too. "That doesn't look friendly."

By now both Austin and Drew had to sprint to stay in front of the surge.

"Not that way, Drew!" One look told Austin they couldn't outrun this thing, whatever it was. "Into one of the shops!"

That would have been a fine idea if any of the doors they tried had been unlocked.

"This is unreal!" Drew tried yet another door without any luck. Two buildings down, though, a window swung open, and a girl popped her head out to look at them.

"Oh, dear. One mustn't be out in the street when the spam comes rolling through," she told them in a proper English accent. Then she pulled back inside and slammed the window shut.

*Thanks for the warning,* Austin thought.

"Wait a minute!" yelled Drew, but Austin knew it was too late. He looked over his shoulder as the rolling blob washed over their ankles, nearly sweeping them off their feet.

From down the street, this flood had sounded like a water-fall. Now it sounded strangely as if they were standing inside the Chiddix gym during a pep assembly with everyone yelling and screaming and stomping and clapping.

*Bam!* Something hit Austin behind the knees and pushed him into a jumbled puddle of words. He slipped on them as he tried to get away, but he managed to stay standing.

"Hey, friend!" The words began speaking as they bubbled up around him. "I lost forty pounds in two weeks. So can you!"

Austin did his best not to fall into what was now a growing river of words. When Drew almost went down, Austin grabbed the back of his friend's shirt as they slogged through another whirlpool.

"This is *not* spam!" it said. "Just forward this e-mail to fifteen friends, and Bill Gates will send you one thousand dollars. It's true!"

"What is this stuff?" Drew tried to keep up with Austin, but making their way down the street was like trying to walk in a flooded creek. Each piece of junk e-mail had a different voice, sometimes jumbled, but most of the time far too easy to understand.

"Triple your money in just three days!" claimed another piece of spam. "As seen on national TV."

Austin felt Drew's shirt start to tear, but he wasn't about to let go.

Another voice sobbed, "Could you spare just ten to twenty minutes of your time to save these poor puppies' lives? The person who sends this to the most people can choose from these two prizes…"

The spam was getting so loud that Austin had to yell into Drew's ear. "We've got to get out of this mess!"

Sure, but how? Yet another junk e-mail now swirled around their legs. "Greetings, I am Enegu Babah. In order to transfer twenty-six million dollars from our bank in Nigeria, I have the courage to ask you, a reliable and honest person—"

"This stuff is making me sick!" Drew yelled back. Come to think of it, his face did look awfully green. Austin figured his own face probably didn't look much better.

*Whap!* A bicycle washed into them from behind, catching Austin's foot. Still he held on as the spam flood washed them farther down the street.

"Incredible, but true! We are giving you two round-trip airline tickets and two free hotel nights in Hawaii, Paris, Florida, or other fabulous vacation destinations."

And then—*swoosh!*—the slippery cobblestones beneath their feet disappeared as if they had stepped straight into a hole. The flood that closed in over their heads dumped them into another Web site with a *thump.*

"Oh," groaned Drew. "I can think of better ways to travel."

*No argument there.* Austin tried to figure out where they'd washed up, but all he could see were some bright lights. One thing was sure: Wherever they were now, it was a long way from Oxford.

# CHAPTER 9

# E-Distress

"Hello?" Ashley was always the first to pick up the Websters' phone, guaranteed. "Oh, hi, Mrs. Scarola…"

As in Drew's mom.

"No, I haven't seen him or Austin since school let out. Maybe they went to the DQ to hang out. Yes ma'am, I heard about the tornado watch being extended. Sure, if I see them, I'll tell Drew you want him home right away."

She hung up her rain slicker and read the note on the kitchen table from her mom: *Running errands—back by 3:00. Cookies on the counter. You can have one or two. Austin, don't eat the leftover pizza. Love, Mom.*

Ashley heard the front screen door squeak open.

"Hey, Austin, where have you been?" she asked without turning around. "Drew's mom just called, and she—"

"Ashley?"

Actually, Ashley was surprised it had taken Jessi so long to stop by. Jessi shook the rain from her long blond hair as she came in.

"Mom almost didn't let me out of the house." Jessi padded into the kitchen to join Ashley. "I reminded her that it's not like you live far away and that it's just a tornado watch. Still, all that tornado stuff on the radio is giving me the creeps too."

"Yeah, I know. Dad's probably on one of his storm alerts at the hospital."

Jessi helped herself to a homemade chocolate-chip cookie and glanced at the kitchen computer when it chirped to announce a new e-mail.

"Probably a very important notice telling us how we can regrow hair for just $19.95 plus tax." Ashley took a bite of her own cookie. "Dad says we need to get a new spam blocker to keep out all that junk."

"This one looks like it's from your brother. Is that spam?"

"Huh?" Ashley leaned over her mother's desk to see what Jessi was talking about. "Why would he be e-mailing us?"

" 'Drew and I are on spam site,' " Jessi read aloud while Ashley skimmed ahead. " 'Laptop in band practice room three in box of coat-drive coats. Probably shut off, so we're stuck. No other way out. Need you to power it back up or your money back.' "

"Uh-oh," Ashley frowned. "I was afraid of something like this."

"What is he talking about with that 'Drew and I' stuff?"

"You know," Ashley told her. "His friend Drew Scarola. The guy who moved here this past summer from Pittsburgh?"

"I know Drew. I just can't believe Austin took him into the Web without even asking us."

"Well, he sent *you*."

"That's different. I went after you. It sounds as if—"

"It sounds as if Austin's gotten himself into trouble again."

"And we girls are going to have to come to the rescue?"

"I just hope this isn't some kind of joke." Ashley sighed and put her coat back on. "I have no idea what that 'or-your-money-back' business was all about."

As they turned to leave, the computer chirped once more.

"It says, 'Ashley, are you there?' " Jessi read aloud. " 'We need to get out of here. Please respond to this special offer.' "

Ashley was already headed out the door. Brothers could be such a pain, but at least the rain had let up for a while.

"Maybe we're out of range," Drew suggested. "Like a cell phone."

"I don't think so." Austin shook his head as they walked across the shiny floor of the new Web site. "We're supposed to be able to link right back to my laptop, but—"

"But what?"

"But it's like my laptop isn't even there. And what's just as weird, I can't even find a link back to the C. S. Lewis site."

"Why don't we just e-mail ourselves back to another computer?" Drew asked.

"I thought of that"—Austin looked down at the endless rows of big black-and-white squares—"but the way I programmed my computer to send us this time, it won't work. We have to go back the way we came, to the same address. It was supposed to be better this way."

"Great." Drew straightened his shirt and tried to fix his hair as best he could, but he still looked like a half-drowned rat. "At least the spam stuff is gone."

"Not all of it." Austin pointed to a wiggling mess of words on the floor off to the left of them that looked like a bowl of alphabet noodles someone had spilled. He stomped on it.

"Visit our site. Win something special!" The words squeaked like a doggy chew toy under Austin's foot.

He stomped again, and the words dribbled out more quietly this time. "You have already won something wonderful!"

One more stomp, and he barely heard a whisper. "Your name was chosen to receive something fabulous..."

And then silence.

*Something fabulous. Yeah right.*

"You think your sister got our cut-and-paste e-mails?" asked Drew. He meant the ones they'd put together from loose pieces of spam a few minutes earlier.

"I'm not sure." Austin looked back at the *Contact Us* link where they had tried to send their messages home.

What else could they do?

"If they do get through," he told Drew, "I hope Ashley gets them before my parents do. They'd freak out."

"Yeah, so would mine, and they will anyway if we don't come home from school. How long do you think it's going to take for your sister to get to your computer?"

"Not quite sure. With this spam mess, things online seem weirder than normal."

"Great. So what does that mean?"

Austin sighed, "I don't know. We could be in here for days. Maybe longer."

Drew was quiet as they kept walking across what seemed like acres of bright flooring, only now they could see blue high-rise buildings in the distance. That gave them something to head toward. Except a few minutes later they found that the high rises weren't high rises at all.

"Cool." Drew craned his neck as he eyed a twenty-foot-tall square can of Spam. "How much of that meat stuff do you think is in one of these things?"

"I have no idea."

"Almost makes me hungry."

"Not me." Austin shuddered while Drew walked all the way around the can as if he were looking for a door—or a can opener.

"Now I really am getting hungry," Drew told him. "There's a recipe on the side of this thing."

"Try not to think about it."

"With all this food around us?"

"We just need to keep moving and listening. And hope we don't hear that waterfall sound again." Austin noticed something new. "You see that?" he asked, pointing. "Look at the links and things in the floor. Photos. Timelines."

"We're lost and we're gonna die, but my buddy is still the trivia king."

"No, really, look." Austin leaned in to see better. "It says Spam was invented in 1937, and a lot of the troops during World War II had it as rations."

"Sounds good to me. You sure there isn't a way into that thing?" Drew was still checking out the huge can. "Maybe I could eat my way right through it."

"Doubt it." Austin was starting to get an idea though. "But look. This may be our ticket out of here and back to where we started."

They watched a short movie of a young woman cooking over a portable stove in a crowded old kitchen.

"You're dreaming." Drew scratched his head. "This is going to get us back home?"

"*Margaret Thatcher Eats Spam During World War II,*" Austin read. "Yep, this is the way to go. Trust me."

"Trust you? That's how I got into this mess in the first place."

# CHAPTER 10

# Prime Suspect

Ashley and Jessi raced up the wet sidewalk to the school, hoping not to get caught in another downpour in their rush to help Austin and Drew. The door opened just as Ashley was reaching for the handle.

Tucker Campbell nearly ran them over, blinded by the two boxes of coats in her arms. "Oh!"

"Sorry." Ashley stood to the side and wondered if she should say anything more. "You need some help with that stuff?"

Ever since the disaster at the Greatest Young Vocalist Competition in July, Tucker had avoided Ashley. Not that they had been good friends before, but things were downright icy now that Tucker thought Austin and Ashley had ruined her chance at fame and fortune.

"Not from you." Tucker pointed her nose into the drizzle and brushed right past them.

Ashley took a close look at the boxes as she walked by.

"Tucker?" Jessi called. "Did you take those coats out of a band practice room?" She must have noticed the same thing as Ashley.

Tucker didn't even slow her pace as she hurried down the walkway toward the parking lot. Mrs. Campbell was waiting at the curb in her silver Lexus.

"What if I did?" she said over her shoulder. "It's for the cheerleaders' fund-raiser."

"Yeah, but—"

"Forget it, Jessi." Ashley pulled her aunt in through the doors. She wasn't in the mood for another catfight with Tucker Campbell. "It's probably not the same box. Austin always locks the practice room when he uses it."

"Then how are we supposed to check it?"

Ashley stopped. "Good question."

They would find out soon enough. The room where Austin practiced his clarinet was just down the hall, to the left and around the corner, through the music room, and...

Unlocked.

"Somebody's already been in here." Jessi checked behind the door, under the piano bench, in the corner, but it was clear there was no computer anywhere. "We should have—"

"Don't say it." Ashley turned an empty box upside down. They should have checked Tucker's load.

Now what?

"Do you still think it's a joke?"

Ashley sat down on the piano bench. She could easily imagine her brother jumping into the Internet without thinking, maybe showing off for his friend and ending up in trouble.

"I don't think so. I think he's stuck, just like the e-mail said. And if we don't get his laptop back from Tucker, he's going to be stuck for a very long time."

It wasn't traveling from link to link that was so hard. It was the landing.

At least the teenage girl was nice enough to help them up off the linoleum kitchen floor.

"Mum!" she called into the next room, a den in the small apartment over a grocery store. "We've visitors for dinner. Two young internauts!"

It sounded as if this kind of thing happened to them every day.

A middle-aged woman stepped into the kitchen, wiping her hands on an apron.

"Well, how do you like that, Maggie. A bit scrawny, perhaps, but they're certainly welcome here. Why don't you dish them each up a plate of Spam?"

Drew didn't waste any time finding a place at the kitchen table, but Austin thought he'd better explain first.

"Uh, thanks so much, but actually we're just lost."

"Lost internauts—and Yanks, too." She seemed to be enjoying this. "Somehow that doesn't surprise me," she chuckled.

"Yes ma'am, and we're looking for a link."

"Well, then why didn't you say so?" The woman pointed at a row of lighted squares along one side of the kitchen floor, totally out of place with the worn gray linoleum and the rest of the 1940s look. This was still a Web site after all. "Can't say that I've ever touched 'em myself, but you're more than welcome to help yourself."

She looked over her shoulder at an easy chair in the den, where a man was mostly hidden behind his newspaper. "Alfred, do you know where any of these links in the kitchen lead to?"

"Eh?" Alfred must have been reading something interesting. "Don't touch those things. You'll lose your programming—or your hair. Don't know which would be worse."

"But it's not for me."

"Doesn't matter. I said—"

"That's all right, ma'am." Austin didn't want to cause an argument. "Maybe it was kind of a bad idea, but I thought I'd be able to find our way back by linking through Margaret Thatcher's life."

"Thatcher?" The girl's mother sounded puzzled. "No wonder you're lost. There's no Margaret Thatcher here. Just Margaret Roberts, though we call her Maggie."

"Oh right. I knew that. See, Thatcher is her married name, and when she becomes the famous prime minister, she's Margaret Thatcher."

At that the girl's face turned beet red, and her dad dropped his paper on the floor.

"Married name," whispered her mother, her lip quivering as she said it.

Her daughter slipped an arm around her mother's shoulder. "It's all right, Mum. I'm still here."

But her mother only shook her head as if dazed.

"Alfred," she croaked, "do we know any young men named Thatcher?"

"Was wondering the same myself." He looked as if he might chew off the end of his unlit pipe when a long, low siren went off in the distance.

# CHAPTER 11

# Maggie, Version 1.1

"Thanks." Ashley swiveled the office phone on the counter so she could dial the number.

The school secretary nodded and turned right back to the radio. "I hope that's your mother you're calling," she told Ashley. "I hear they may have sighted a tornado four or five counties away."

As bad as that news was, Ashley had another emergency on her mind. Jessica pointed to the name in the phone book: *Campbell, Tucker G.* The girl had her own phone number, and she answered on the second ring.

"Tucker Campbell speaking. How may I help you?"

Anybody else would have just said, "Hello." Ashley almost hung up, but she had to know.

"Uh, Tucker, this is Ashley...Webster."

There was silence on the other end as Ashley went on.

"Look, I think Austin might have left his laptop in one of

the piles of coats for the drive, and you might have taken it home...by accident."

"His *laptop?* Well, if it's missing, maybe it serves him right for bringing it to school. Isn't there a rule against that?"

"He has special permission. But look, do you think you could check the pile of coats you have? It's super important."

"You want me to do *you* a favor?"

"Whatever you want to call it. It's life or death." Ashley took a deep breath. Austin was going to owe her big time. "Please?"

"Ah, this is sweet. So after what you did to me, you're begging for help?"

Ashley tried to think of something nice to say back, but it was getting harder and harder.

"Listen, you don't know how important this is," she finally replied. "All I'm asking is for you to check in between the coats, and we'll come get the laptop. It's no skin off your nose."

Jessi leaned in closer to hear what was going on.

"Why doesn't Austin ask me himself?"

"Tell her just to give it back!" hissed Jessi.

"I heard that," Tucker snapped. "But what was your brother doing hiding his computer in a bunch of coats anyway?"

"It's none of your business." Jessi snatched the phone from Ashley. "Just give it back right now."

"Oooo!" Tucker was screaming by this time, and Ashley could almost feel the heat of her anger over the phone. "How dare you accuse me of stealing!"

Ashley took back the phone. "We're not accusing you of anything, Tucker. It's just that—"

"And even if I *had* found it, maybe I wouldn't tell you!"

*Click.*

Ashley knew the sound of someone hanging up. She sighed and closed her eyes.

"That's what I was afraid of."

Jessi, though, was already charging for the office door, muttering the whole way. Glued to the tornado reports, the secretary didn't even seem to notice they were leaving.

"She has it. I just know she does." Jessi held the door open, waiting for Ashley to catch up. "And we're going to get it."

Everyone in the little apartment at *www.margaretthatcher.org* scrambled when they heard the wail of the sirens.

"German air raid?" Austin wanted to know.

"Used to be." Maggie grabbed a sweater off a hook. "Lately it's spam."

Drew groaned.

"That's it!" Mr. Roberts sprang to action, grabbing a dented World War I helmet from the shelf and exchanging his worn slippers for rubber boots. "Everyone into the Anderson."

"What's an Anderson?" asked Drew.

"A backyard air-raid shelter," replied Maggie. "Built from a kit. Daddy buried it in the little garden behind the shop, and we planted lovely flowers over the top."

"Whoa, hang on." Drew stuffed the last of his dinner into his mouth. "Caves give me the creeps."

"Come on, now!" Mr. Roberts waved at them from the door. "We don't have much time."

"Thanks for dinner, Mrs. Roberts, but I think we'd better keep going," Austin decided.

"Well, then, God bless you. The links are yours to use." She paused at her door for just a moment with her hand on her daughter's shoulder. "Our Maggie's really going to be the PM, you say? Fancy that!"

"Let's go, Beatrice!" Mr. Roberts hurried them down the stairs to the underground air-raid shelter as the sound of a waterfall grew louder.

"We've heard *that* before." Austin tried not to panic, but he couldn't tell which link would take them back the way they had come, back to C. S. Lewis.

*Biography*? Maybe.

*Speeches?* He didn't think so.

*Quotes?* Drew was looking that one over, but Austin wasn't so sure.

*Her Years at Oxford?*

"That's it!" Austin clapped his hands. The Roberts's home was now shaking as the spam approached. "This will take us back to Oxford!"

That would have been good, except Drew was on his hands and knees, looking down into the *Quotes* link.

"I see something here," he said. "I think she likes to read C. S. Lewis. She said—"

Well, that might have been a good link to try too, but by that time the spam flood had surrounded them.

*Slam!* The first wave crushed into the den where Mr. Roberts had been reading his paper. A second later, spam surrounded Austin's ankles.

"I promise you that everyone who forwards this message will be in the *Guinness Book of World Records!*"

That was all they could stand to hear. Austin was already stepping into his link when Drew gave up on his and dived to join him.

# CHAPTER 12

# The Reverend Spoo

"Ah, that's more like it."

Austin relaxed on a bench in the front row of a small chapel full of college students wearing dark blazers and ties. The students were all guys, but that was fine with Austin. The one next to him poked him in the ribs.

"Here it comes," he whispered. "He's sure to deliver one of his lines soon."

Austin looked up at the speaker to see what his neighbor meant. In the pulpit a smallish, pink-faced man with white hair peered through thick glasses at his audience and then down again at the podium in front of him. By the way he talked, he seemed to be wrapping up his speech.

"Once again, I can only remind you young men of the words we read in First Corinthians, chapter thirteen, the twelfth verse: 'For now we see through a dark, glassly, but then...'"

The guy next to Austin would have burst out laughing if he hadn't put a cork in it. "Through a glass darkly" had become "through a dark glassly," which wouldn't have been that funny, except it was coming from a serious-looking, seventy-something gentleman standing in the pulpit.

A see-through sign that was large enough for everyone to see popped up behind his head, but the speaker ignored it. This was a Web site, after all, and pop-ups were part of the landscape.

Across the top in bright red letters it read, *Top Ten Spoonerisms. Number one (spoken to a school secretary): "Is the bean dizzy?"*

Okay. Austin was getting to start it. Whoops, that would be starting to get it.

*Number two (spoken to a lazy student): "You have hissed all of my mystery lectures."*

"Is that C. S. Lewis?" whispered Drew a little too loudly.

A few students looked at them and snickered.

"I should think internauts like you would know better," one of them whispered back. "That's Spoo."

*Spoo?*

"The Reverend W. A. Spooner to you, young man." Whatever else the students thought of their speaker, the man had keen hearing. And he wasn't finished quite yet. "Stand, please, for the final hymn."

The whisperer grinned but hung his head as they all got to their feet.

The reverend winked at Austin.

"Number 237, please. 'Kinkering Congs Their Titles Take.'"

That was Spoonerism number three on the list, and it blinked when the words came out of his mouth. Austin held his hymnal up to cover his grin as they sang. It wasn't hard to see why the guys in the chapel were waiting for the man to slip up. And while he was not quite sure what time in the history of Oxford this was on the Web site, at least they were in the right place.

Who knows? Maybe Rev. Spooner could show them the way to C. S. Lewis.

Ten minutes later the man was rubbing his chin, as if thinking over an answer to their question.

"Lewis, you say?" He shook his head. "Of course. He's currently a student at University College, though in the future he will go on to become one of Christianity's most respected thinkers."

"That's him!" Austin was glad they were getting closer.

"Of course, Oxford is made up of twenty-nine different colleges and is attended by thousands of students. It won't be easy to find him. And even if you do, remember he's still a student here. Your young Mr. Lewis may not have much to tell you."

He must have seen how their faces fell.

"There, there, not to worry. I'll show you around the campus. We have plenty of time before dinner. If you're really that interested in this chap Lewis, perhaps you'd like to see his portrait on the Wall of Heroes."

"I thought you said he was still just a student here," Austin said.

"Quite right. But the site programmers have been a little...creative. This is the Internet, after all."

So they followed Rev. Spooner down the halls, learning that he was not only a reverend but also a professor and the warden of the college.

"You Americans would call me the college president," he added with a smile as he led them around a corner. And there on the walnut-paneled wall, dozens of portraits showed famous past, present, and even future Oxford students.

"William Penn, 1662," read Austin as he walked by one of the first life-size portraits. "Founder of Pennsylvania." The painting shimmered in a way he'd never seen before, as if the paint hadn't dried yet. He reached out to touch the canvas, but his finger disappeared into it with an odd sucking sound.

*Whoa.* He pulled back the finger, still attached. *How about another finger?* Same thing. But this time the painting tugged him in all the way up to the wrist before he yanked it back.

"Say, Reverend," he asked, "is there something different about these paintings?"

"And up there," continued the reverend, "is Jonathan Swift, who wrote *Gulliver's Travels;* J. R. R. Tolkien, who will write as well—several fantasies about rings; and Theodore Geisel, who will become a wonderful writer for children in a few years. I believe you'll know him as Dr. Seuss."

"No kidding?" Now Drew seemed interested. "The guy who wrote *How the Grinch Stole Christmas* went to college here?"

"Presidents, princes, prime ministers, poets, playwrights, and politicians all scum to this cool...er...come to this school. This is a fine institution."

"This guy, too?" Drew pointed to a stern-looking fellow. He must not have noticed what had happened to Austin's hand earlier. And actually, it all happened so fast that Austin couldn't have stopped it.

"Er...I wouldn't touch that!" Rev. Spooner tried to warn him, but too late. "These links are..."

Austin couldn't even get a hand on him before the painting sucked Drew in.

"...active." The reverend finished his sentence.

Active links? Austin should have guessed. Now Drew had disappeared the way the last noodle is sucked in by a hungry spaghetti eater.

"Oh, dear." Rev. Spooner frowned. "I never have quite understood what happens after that."

"Where did he go?"

"Well, the portrait is of William Tyndale. I believe it was done when the man was in exile, hiding in Antwerp."

"You mean Antwerp, Belgium?" Austin wasn't on the Chiddix Knowledge Bowl team for nothing.

"The country eventually became known as Belgium, yes. It was still part of the Low Countries in the early 1500s." He launched into a sixty-second lecture on Mr. Tyndale, a famous Oxford student from that time.

"That's great, sir, but…" Austin wasn't sure how much he had to know before jumping in after Drew. He wasn't even sure if he'd end up in the same place.

But he was about to find out.

# CHAPTER 13

# Just a Peek

"This is not a good idea," Ashley whispered from her spot in the bushes next to Jessi, under the spreading branches of a very old oak tree in Tucker Campbell's side yard. "In fact, this is nuts. We could get arrested for this."

"Perfect. Then we can tell the police all about Tucker the thief."

"She's not a thief if she didn't know she was taking the laptop."

"Yeah, but we told her—"

"I know, I know." Ashley shook her head. "But that's not going to help us now. What if a neighbor sees us peeking in Tucker's window and calls the police?"

"You see how dark it's getting? Nobody's going to see us— as long as you keep quiet."

Jessi was right about it being dark. Come to think of it,

though, that was the weird part: Four in the afternoon, and it seemed as dark as night.

"Come on, Miss Gymnast." Jessi waved at the light filtering down from the first-floor window, which sat higher than usual thanks to the home's lookout basement. "All you have to do is balance on my shoulders to see inside. I'll bet she's sitting right there with Austin's laptop, ready to smash it with a hammer or something."

"She wouldn't!" But Ashley knew that, as bizarre as it sounded, Tucker might. She sighed. She'd take just a peek, and then they would run as fast as they could back home.

At that moment the clouds opened up the way they do only once or twice a year, when the rain flattens everything it touches, turning the streets to rivers and drawing a solid curtain of water down on everything. And here they were, standing right out in the middle of the downpour. It would probably serve them right if they were struck by one of the bolts of lightning that let loose without warning.

Ashley did her best to crawl up on Jessi's shoulders to see over the window ledge. She thought she heard Tucker's annoying laugh from the other side of the window. She was probably on the phone in there, hopefully not looking out the window at the growing storm. If anyone saw them... Well, Ashley had never been to jail before. Oh so slowly, she inched her face up against the window to get a look. But with so much rain now pelting the glass, everything had clouded up. Through the haze, she saw someone who looked like Tucker pacing around the room. She also saw a desk with a glowing light that looked a lot like the screen of a laptop. Then Mrs. Campbell called to Tucker from somewhere inside the house—loudly enough to be heard over the pouring rain.

Suddenly the inside lights flickered, and it wasn't from the lightning.

"Ash," Jessi whispered up at her. "You're getting heavy. See anything?"

That's when something else made Ashley look around. It was the sound of Niagara Falls and a hundred trucks all at the same time. Since when had Tucker Campbell's house been moved to the middle of Interstate 55?

"Let me down." Being up on her aunt's shoulders was the last place Ashley wanted to be. A moment later they were both sprawling on their backs in the Campbells' soggy side lawn, being bombarded with rain that stung their cheeks like bees.

"Maybe we need to go home," Jessi told her.

Yeah, being outside in a storm like this, even to help Austin, was about as dumb as could be. And Ashley was ready to agree until she got to her knees. Her heart stopped as she looked down the street.

"Do you see what I see?" She had to raise her voice to be

heard over the growing roar and the sirens that had started up all around them.

For the longest second they both stared, like two mice staring at a cobra about to have them for lunch. Oh sure, Ashley had seen tornadoes on The Weather Channel and on the weather-safety training videos they'd had to watch at school. A number of times she'd even huddled in the school tornado shelters during the occasional spring tornado warnings. But the tornadoes—if they came at all—were always somewhere else in the state.

Not this time.

Black and dangerous, the tornado's shape kept changing every second, looking not at all like the friendly, cartoon-style tornado she'd always imagined. Lightning flashed around it in the murky green darkness like a strobe light. The funnel chilled Ashley to the core as it dropped out of the cloud, moving ever closer to the ground as it barreled straight at them.

# CHAPTER 14

# Where's Tyndale?

"This isn't right." Austin stood in a shadowy cobblestone lane, lost before he began. He caught a faint glimmer of the Web address up in the corner—*www.williamtyndale.com*—but nothing more.

What had happened to Drew?

He noticed a woman watching him from a tiny window in the side of a crooked, two-story house attached to hundreds of other crooked little houses and shops, all crammed into this bustling Web site of wandering alleyways and dead-end mazes.

"I need to find my friend Drew," he told the woman. "He's kind of dressed like me, except shorter with dark hair. Oh, and he's wearing a pair of Nikes."

The woman pulled the window shut, muttering in a strange language that didn't sound French and wasn't quite German. Obviously the translation feature wasn't plugged into this Web site.

"Thanks anyway," he told her as he tried to figure out what type of site this latest link had brought him to. He jumped out of the way—just barely—when another woman dumped a stinky-smelling bucket of kitchen scraps onto the street from an upper window.

At least he thought it was kitchen scraps at first, but when he looked down at the gutter, he groaned.

"Not that spam stuff again."

"Oh yes," said a child's voice in reply. "Please forward this e-mail to everyone in your address book and then contact Mrs. Burrard's fifth-grade class so we can put a pin in the map by your city. We want to see how many people we can reach in just thirty days."

It was actually a nice idea, except those chain letters always seemed to get a little out of hand. In a way, though, the chain letter reminded him of what Rev. Spooner had told him about William Tyndale, the father of the English Bible who had wanted to get the Scriptures to as many regular people as he could. Knowledge Bowl Factoid: He had translated the Bible into English, but that had gotten him into big trouble with King Henry VIII. In fact, Tyndale had to run for his life when the king tried to have him arrested, which probably explained why he was nowhere to be seen on the streets of this Web site.

But never mind all that now. It was time to find Drew and get out of there. Austin hustled through the busy streets, watching his step as he went. Every block or so he cupped his hands and yelled as loudly as he could.

"DREW!"

His shouts echoed through the alleys, but no Drew. So he tried something else.

"MR. TYNDALE!"

Again, no answer. Of course, Tyndale was probably hiding and wouldn't be easy to find.

Another bucket of junk e-mail came flying out of the sky, splattering so the words broke apart on the wet cobblestones.

Austin heard a shout, and from around the corner a small, mixed-breed dog came galloping right at him. Make that two.

Or ten. A bread roll dangled from the lead dog's mouth, which the rest of the yelping pack probably would have liked to share. And right behind them was Drew.

"Austin!" Drew hollered. "Stop him!"

Drew must have been awfully hungry to be chasing dogs for his lunch. Austin planted himself in the middle of the very narrow lane, a foot on each side. But as the dog flew at him, it didn't slow down. It zipped right between Austin's legs, knocking him over.

"Oomph!" Austin tumbled backward against the wall of a shop. Behind him the lane turned into a covered walkway just wide enough for one skinny person—and the dogs—to squeeze through. Austin turned around and found himself looking into the knees of a stern-looking man in puffy, Christopher Columbus–style pants and a brimmed metal helmet with two pointed ends. The man held a serious-looking club in both hands, ready for action.

"Er...sorry." Austin dusted off his pants as he scrambled back to his feet. "I was just, uh...we were just visiting."

The guard frowned and looked straight ahead.

"You let that thief run right by you!" Drew told a second guard at the other end of the walkway. Instead of a club, this man held a coil of rope.

Austin figured it would be a good idea to move on. "Drew, they don't speak English." He tried to pull his friend away. "Nobody on this site speaks English. Let's—"

But the guard with the club stepped forward.

"Eeng-leesh?" His face darkened.

*Uh-oh.* Austin held up his hands, palms out.

"No, no." Drew shook his head as if to make sure the guy got the message. Then he pointed to Austin and himself. "American. We're from Normal, Illinois. By Chicago? I've never even been to England, except for on the Internet, and that doesn't really count, right?"

Blank stares. The guards looked at each other and shrugged.

"Drew, forget it." Austin walked him through the narrow, dark passageway till they came out by a little lace shop on the other side. "This Web site is supposed to show Antwerp in 1535. Think about it. Where's Chicago in 1535?"

"Guess that's a couple of years before my time."

"Mine, too."

"But, Tyndale…is he the guy in the painting?" Drew asked. "You yelled his name."

If they could find Tyndale, Austin explained as they threaded through the crowds and the narrow streets, maybe they could find a way out, too. After all, the Web site was named for him, so probably the best links were clustered around wherever he was.

"Pardon me." A man came up through the crowd behind them. "But I couldn't help overhearing."

And Austin couldn't help noticing that somebody was finally speaking English. He and Drew turned to see a man smiling at them from behind a pointed beard that was sharpened at the chin. Except for the beard, he looked awfully familiar, though Austin couldn't quite place the face.

"You're a friend of William Tyndale's?" the bearded man asked.

"Well…" Austin wasn't sure how to answer. "Not exactly."

But by that time the man had nodded to someone else in the crowd, and Austin felt a rough hand grab his arm from behind.

# CHAPTER 15

# Little Web Guide Who Could

"Hey!" Austin yelled his protest, but no one in the crowd seemed to notice. "You're twisting my arm!"

Well, *that* did a lot of good. The thug nearly squeezed Austin to death as he pushed both Austin and Drew up against the side of a building. This guy had quite the grip for a digital character.

"You're here to save him, aren't you?" The man who had approached them moments ago through the crowd now sneered in Austin's face. "Admit it! You internauts are always on a mission."

"Well...I couldn't just leave him here." Austin wasn't sure what the man was getting at.

"Finally, the truth!" The man crossed his arms. "A friend of William Tyndale the heretic."

"Wait a minute." Austin wasn't sure how to get out of this one. "I was talking about my friend Drew here."

"A friend of Tyndale's is no friend of King Henry's"—the man wasn't listening—"and shall be dealt with most severely."

"I never even *heard* of William Tyndale until maybe an hour ago." Drew squirmed, but it only made the big guy clamp down even harder on both of them. "But I have seen *you* somewhere before though."

"Liars both! I heard you talking, even calling his name."

"You don't understand." Austin could see that arguing with this guy was pointless. He looked up and saw a girl push open a window right above their heads. But this time he didn't yell or try to jump to the side until the bucketful of spam hit them squarely on their heads.

"Ay!" The muscleman loosened his grip for just a second, but that was long enough. Austin was ready, and he shoved Drew to the side with him.

"Wonder diet pills really work!" shouted the spam as it clung to the men in a mass. "I lost forty-five pounds in…"

Austin and Drew didn't stay to hear more. They slipped through the fish sellers and shoppers as fast as they could.

"They're getting away, Master Philips!" cried the thug.

"I need them back here!" shouted Philips. "Before they can do any damage! And watch to see if the taller one picks up a small, flat box somewhere."

Austin didn't know what on earth Philips was talking about, but he and Drew slipped between two shops and kept moving, sometimes sprinting down alleys and stairways, sometimes climbing across roofs and up ladders.

Well, if they weren't lost before, they were now. They stopped to catch their breath, hands on their knees, gasping and looking around them. Nothing looked familiar.

"Did we"—Drew gasped—"lose 'em?"

"I think so." But a tug on the back of Austin's shirt made him jump.

"Lost, English internaut friends? I can show you around!" A little boy looked up at them with the widest gap-toothed grin Austin had ever seen. He couldn't have been older than seven or eight, tops, which meant he had to look up, even to Drew.

"Where did you come from?" Austin asked him.

"I'm Willy," the boy shrugged. "Live here in Antwerp and work as a tour guide for the Web."

"Aren't you a little small to be doing this kind of thing?" Drew wondered aloud.

"You're not too big yourself."

"Okay," Drew laughed. "And I thought everybody around here only spoke Belgian. But you—"

"No such thing as Belgian." Willy planted his hands on his hips while a cluster of flags appeared above his head, making a *ffffit-ffffit-ffffit* sound. "It's Flemish. And besides that and English, I speak five other languages: French, Dutch, Spanish, Italian, and Russian."

"Sounds like you know a little of everything." Austin glanced around to be sure Philips and his pal hadn't caught up to them. "So how fast can you find us William Tyndale?"

"Depends. You a friend of his?"

Where had they just heard that question?

"We haven't met him yet," said Austin. "But we need to… Well, it's a long story. We're not his enemies, if that's what you're wondering."

"Hmm." Willy appeared to size them up; then he held out his hand, palm up. "Okay, but I don't work for free, you know."

Drew groaned. "I knew there was a catch."

"No catch," Willy told them. "Just fair pay."

"Okay, here." Austin handed him a dollar from the lunch money he hadn't spent. "How about American cash?"

"American. Hmm." Willy studied the bill, held it up to the light, then slipped it into his pocket. "Don't know what that is, but it'll do for now. Follow me."

Easy for him to say. Willy seemed to lead them through every side alley and lane in the ancient city, past shops and into an open square with a stone church on one end.

"He's a nice guy, Tyndale." Willy looked back at them as he continued on. "You sure you're not after him like Philips?"

"You know Philips?" Austin stopped the Web guide.

"Sure, I do." He spit at Austin's feet. "Wanted me to guide them to Tyndale when he's not at the house where he stays so they can burn him at the stake."

Austin shivered at the thought. Maybe he'd seen a picture of this Philips character in one of his history books.

"Philips is an internaut like you two," added Willy.

"Wait a minute." Austin was surprised at that. "But Philips looks as blurry as everybody else on the Internet, not at all sharp like Drew and me."

"Yeah, some internauts can do that—make themselves blurry so people here won't know. But I know. See?" Willy pointed across the square, and where he pointed, a small bubble of text popped up to explain.

*This is the home of English merchants in Antwerp,* read the bubble. *Tyndale was invited to stay here at this safe house in 1534, where he could continue his translating work.*

"Okay, I saw the bubble, but I don't see anybody." Austin strained his eyes looking.

"And I don't get what's so criminal about translating the Bible," said Drew.

Willy pressed his lips together and shook his head.

"Look closer," he told them. "There goes Tyndale again with that snake Philips, thinking he's off to a luncheon."

They heard one of the men laughing in the distance, and that's when it clicked. That laugh…

"Mr. Z!" Austin whispered. Mr. Z was dressed up as Philips, and it was a pretty good costume. But why was he here? And where was he going with Tyndale?

Their guide pointed at the two men as another bubble popped up.

*Henry Philips introduced himself as a friendly English businessman who agreed with what Tyndale was doing. But he was really a sort of hired thug for the English king. He tricked Tyndale into leaving the safety of the merchants' house, where the Bible translator was ambushed in a narrow street by two armed men. After nearly one and a half years in the dungeon at Vilvoorde Castle, William Tyndale was strangled and burned at the stake in Brussels on October 6, 1536. His last words were, "Lord, open the King of England's eyes."*

"Oh no you don't!" Austin couldn't help shouting. He didn't think for a second about changing the way people saw history by messing up the site; he just hadn't liked what he'd read. So he sprinted down the street after the two men as fast as his feet would take him.

# CHAPTER 16

# The Real Thing

Ashley didn't wonder if it would be odd for Tucker Campbell to find them knocking at her front door. She didn't stop to think. Not with the tornado roaring straight for them, threatening to touch down on their heads.

Actually, they didn't even take the time to knock. Jessi burst in through the unlocked front door, and they both tumbled inside.

"Tucker!" Ashley shouted. The house was a lot newer than her own and was laid out differently, so she couldn't find the stairway to the basement right away. But there had to be one. A small TV in the kitchen blared the tornado warning, and a kettle of pasta on the stove was boiling over.

"We're getting several sightings now of three funnel clouds in Logan and McLean Counties," said a nervous-looking young TV newscaster. "This is the real thing. If you live in Bloomington or Normal, you're advised to take cover immediately. Stay off the roads. Get off the phone. Take shelter in the nearest—"

"No time for that!" Ashley knew they had seconds, not minutes. Jessi yanked open a closet door, trying to find the stairway. If they didn't find it quickly, well...

Ashley took a big breath and screamed, "TUCKER!"

Even with the growing roar outside, a muffled shout from below told them all they needed to know.

Ashley found the right door this time, and a moment later they were falling down a carpeted stairway into the Campbells' basement rec room. The door slammed behind them louder than a gunshot.

"My goodness, girls." Former Miss Illinois Mrs. Campbell looked quite a bit more rumpled and uncombed than Ashley had ever seen her. "What are you—I mean, are you all right?"

Ashley just pointed up.

"We saw...a funnel cloud," she gasped. "We were outside, and it was coming—"

No need to explain anything else as they huddled on the carpet next to Tucker and her mom, underneath the stairs past the Foosball table and the big-screen TV. Ashley felt her ears pop, the same feeling she'd once had flying. The roar got even louder, and a big *CRASH!* upstairs made them all jump as if a bomb had landed right above their heads. Jessi yelped and

Tucker shuddered. When Ashley looked over, she could see tears streaming down the other girl's face in the faint glow of a battery-powered night-light.

Ashley put her arm around Tucker's shaking shoulders and held on tightly. In just these few seconds, Tucker the scheming enemy who had stolen her brother's laptop had become Tucker the scared kid next to her who didn't want to get blown away by a tornado either.

"We'll be okay, Tucker." Once the words were out of her mouth, maybe Ashley could believe them too. "God's not done with us yet."

"I'm so glad I finally caught up to you two." Raven Zawisto-kowski, also known as Henry Philips, turned to greet them. "Our instruments tracked you here, but I was starting to worry that they were wrong."

Now that Austin knew the truth, it wasn't hard to see through Mr. Z's disguise. But the two soldiers had already overpowered William Tyndale and tied up his hands and feet by the time Drew came sliding to a stop.

"Don't do that to him, Mr. Z!" Austin demanded. "He didn't do anything to you."

"Boys." Mr. Tyndale looked at them with a sad expression

on his face. "I appreciate your wanting to help, but you can't—"

"He's right." Mr. Z interrupted as he turned to them. "We had our fun playing our parts, but we can't change what really happens at *www-dot-williamtyndale-dot-com,* can we? What happened is history, after all."

"You don't care about changing things," said Austin, standing as tall as he could stand. "Not if you work with Ms. Blankenskrean."

"You're a smart kid." He smiled through his quick look of surprise. "But let me explain something."

"Sure, explain how you mess up the Internet. How you erase and change everything that has to do with faith and the Bible and…"

Mr. Z looked away for a minute. And when he turned back, he wasn't smiling.

"My boss is very good at what she does, but sometimes people don't understand what she's trying to do."

"I understand all right. That's the problem." Austin wasn't backing down.

Mr. Z held up his hands as if trying to settle him down.

"Austin, Austin. We can't change history. This is just a Web site, remember? All I change are a few words here and there, and pretty soon I'm…*improving* the way you see and understand things. Is that so bad?"

"What did you change this time?" Drew wanted to know.

"I promise you, not a thing." Mr. Z nodded at the guards. "Not this time. My only job today was to catch up with you. To make sure you're safe."

"What about your costume?" asked Drew.

"I just thought I'd have a little fun along the way." He held up his arms to better show off the long, puffy sleeves. "Looks just like a real English merchant's outfit, doesn't it?"

Five more soldiers came up from behind. Slipping away wasn't going to be easy.

"Seriously, though," Mr. Z continued. "I'm very sorry you don't *seem* to have your laptop with you. That would have been so much easier."

"Easier for you to steal, you mean." Austin wasn't afraid to say it.

"Goodness! You really don't like me, do you? But listen. I don't think you understand how dangerous your computer would be in here. I'd be happy to place it in safekeeping for you. Or your camera, for that matter."

Austin just glared at him, and Mr. Z motioned for the guards.

"Well, we'll take care of this matter one way or the other. I promised Mattie." He walked over to William Tyndale, still bound. "And I don't think you'd like to spend the next eighteen months with your Internet friend in Vilvoorde Castle. Heard of it?"

Austin didn't move as the soldiers closed in. "You're crazy," he whispered.

"Oh, come on." Mr. Z grinned once again. "Just looking out for you. And the guards will help you, ah, *locate* your missing equipment. You're sure that camera isn't in your pocket?"

So Mr. Z was either going to get Austin's laptop and camera, or he was going to make sure they didn't get back out to use them...for a long time. Was that what he was threatening? No way was Austin going to sit by and let this happen!

"YAAA!" Willy came running down the street, yelling at the top of his lungs. He swung a big stick over his head as he ran, catching one of the guards in the back. William Tyndale fell to the ground and rolled. That took out his guard for a moment, leaving just five more and Mr. Z. Another guard grabbed Willy by the waist, but Willy managed to squirm over to Austin.

"The doors!" he whispered, nodding toward a row of small shops four paces away. "Go for the doors!"

Austin didn't wait around for a better idea. As Mr. Z grabbed for them, he and Drew dived for the nearest shop door, pushed it open, and tumbled inside.

Another link!

Drew and Austin both stared at the blurry guards now dissolving just outside the door. They looked like the fish Austin had seen the time he dived into Lake Winnebago without goggles.

Quickly Austin locked the door before anyone made a move to follow. At least they could catch their breath for a few minutes in this cozy library before Mr. Z decided to come after them.

And he would, wouldn't he?

"I'm confused," said Drew. "I thought we escaped into a shop on a street in Anteater."

"An-*twerp*." Austin corrected him.

Drew looked hurt. "You don't have to call me names just because we're lost again."

# CHAPTER 17

# Webrarian

"I wouldn't say you were lost, boys." A middle-aged man behind a large walnut desk kept his eyes on his computer monitor as he spoke to Austin and Drew. "I can tell you precisely where we are."

"Where's that?" asked Austin.

"Welcome to Michael J. Tyndale's *www-dot-weird-words-workshop-dot-org,* where we explore the meaning and origin of really important words like *flibbertigibbet* and *jobbernowl, kerfuffle* and *mulligrubs, snollygoster* and—"

"Those are words?" Drew broke in.

"Most assuredly. If you like, I can tell you what they mean and explain where they came from. A *snollygoster,* for example—"

"Arg!" Austin hit his forehead. "No offense, it's just that we've been wading through a lot of words lately, what with the spam floods and all."

"Ah, but not like these. Now, take the word *snollygoster*, for example, which means a fast-talking sneak who's always trying to get his own way. Know anyone like that?"

Both boys looked toward the door.

"I thought so." The man nodded as if he understood. He looked harmless enough with his reading glasses propped on his forehead and old books piled in stacks around his desk. "Now, I don't mean to bore you with my hobby, but you are welcome here. Stay as long as you want and leave whenever you like. You'll be safe for a bit."

Austin hoped the man was right; he wasn't looking forward to jumping from site to site, trying to stay one step ahead of the NCCC. What if he never got offline? Would they keep chasing him forever? Austin tried to forget all that by looking at books for a while, mostly odd stories about how words were created and translated. Austin learned that a *flibbertigibbet* was an airhead, and that reminded him of Jessi. The word itself had been around since about 1450, and Shakespeare had come up with the spelling. *Mulligrubs,* on the other hand, was the blues, and it came from the old French word for a headache. And a *kerfuffle?* That was two funny old Scottish words put together. It meant a confused mess—like the one they were in now.

At least now he knew four new words that might come in handy for the Knowledge Bowl, if anyone ever asked. Drew, on the other hand, was over in the corner of the room watching Chad Spaminelli deliver the news on *www.YourWeb Weather.com*. As before, the Web weatherman had popped up out of nowhere.

"The weather guy says there's still lots of spam coming our way," Drew told them. "A couple of systems moving together could produce a superflood."

Michael J. Tyndale looked toward the window and frowned. "I've hardly been able to go outside for days, no thanks to the spam."

He returned to his work, and Austin asked if he could send an e-mail to help them out of this kerfuffle.

The man shrugged. "It's worth a try," he told Austin. "This isn't the 1500s, you know. Even with all the spam floods, I still have my high-speed connection."

But not a high-speed connection to Austin@Austin Web13.com. The word librarian scratched his head after trying the address three times.

"Odd. The e-mail just bounces right back to us. Are you sure that's a good address?"

"Positive. And it's our only way out."

"Would you like me to keep trying?" asked the man.

"Thanks." Austin nodded, but he had to admit that it wasn't looking good. Ashley should have read their other e-mail by now and turned his laptop back on.

"Wait a minute." Drew stopped in front of the desk. "Did you say earlier your name was Tyndale?"

Mr. Tyndale smiled, and when he did, it reminded Austin of the man they had seen on the streets of Antwerp.

"I did. And yes, I do have the same name as the famous Bible translator, which is probably how you found the link here. I'd like to say we're related way back somewhere, but I cannot say for certain. Of course, just about everything is tied together somehow, especially—"

A rap on the door cut him off. Austin and Drew looked at each other, but Mr. Tyndale didn't look nervous at all. He reached into his stack of books and handed a small one to Austin.

"Before you go, this is for you."

Austin read the front page of the little book Tyndale had placed in his hand. *The newe Testament as it was written, and caused to be written, by them which herde yt. To whom also oure saveoure Christ Jesus commanded that they shulde preache it unto al creatures.*

Austin looked up, his question showing on his face.

"A copy of Tyndale's 1526 edition," answered the man. "Since you've met him—or the Internet version, at least—I thought you might like to see how he translated all those words. It was quite an amazing thing he did."

This time the pounding on the door was louder.

"Wow, thanks!" Austin might have a tough time reading the rest of it, but the New Testament was still a cool gift. "Now I think we'd better—"

"I think you'd better too. And I'll keep trying your e-mail address. Can't promise anything, but I'll keep trying. I'd suggest you put the book in your pocket for safekeeping."

Austin did, while Drew peeked out a front window.

"It's him!"

*Bam, bam, bam!*

Austin wasn't sure why it had taken Mr. Z so long to catch up with them. Maybe there was only one door into this link. Or was there?

"Go ahead and pick up any book over there." Mr. Tyndale pointed to a far shelf. "Quickly. Just open it up and leave it on the desk. Each one is a link, you see? Just be careful out there. I'll take care of the snollygoster at the door."

Austin paused for a moment, then picked up a biography of a woman named Harriet Beecher Stowe. Drew had picked up a book of his own too, this one about Bible translators. There wasn't time to look for anything that might bring them closer to home. They knew they couldn't stay there, not with Mr. Z about to burst through the door.

"No, no! Just one link!" Mr. Tyndale warned them—but too late.

# CHAPTER 18

# Seeing Double

It took Austin a moment to adjust to their new site—or rather, *sites*. As soon as they got used to one, everything went totally fuzzy and switched over to the other. From a man sitting behind a laptop at a picnic table in the jungle to a little woman in a dark dress marching up the steps of the White House in Washington, D.C.

And back again.

Problem was, Austin couldn't quite focus on either scene, and he guessed Drew couldn't either. They passed each other coming and going, like riding a spinning, out-of-control merry-go-round, faster and faster, until Austin was dizzy.

No wonder Michael J. Tyndale had wanted them to choose only one of the links. Two was one too many to handle. And here came Drew again, waving his arms.

This time around Austin thought maybe he'd try to tackle his friend to keep him from flying off to the other site. As they picked up speed, Austin stepped to his left. Drew stepped to his right, but not fast enough. And…

*BAM!*

The crash knocked Austin off his feet—and the wind out of him besides. He had to sit for a minute to figure out where they were and what had just happened.

"Ow!" whispered Drew. "I don't care how much money they make, I am never going to be a crash-test dummy when I grow up."

"I hear you," Austin nodded.

At least now they were together in one place. The woman Austin had seen hurrying into the White House stopped for a moment to bend over them.

"Are you boys all right?" she asked, stooping low.

A man in a blue Union army uniform stood at the door, rolling his eyes.

"The president's a busy man, Mrs. Stowe," he called. "I'm sure these clumsy internauts can take care of themselves."

"We'll be right there, lieutenant."

"But ma'am, it's not safe out here. We've had reports of another spam storm coming this way."

"I said I'd be right there. Mr. Lincoln was good enough to wait all this time for me; I'm sure he won't mind waiting just a moment more."

So the lieutenant stood by the door with his arms crossed

while the woman helped Austin and Drew to their feet. She'd probably done the same thing for her own children more than a few times.

"Thanks," Austin said as they made their way to the White House door, where two more blue-coated soldiers stood with rifles ready. Austin remembered seeing guys dressed like that once at a U.S. Civil War Web site.

"Wow," whispered Drew. "We've gone from Bible translator to word-history library to…"

"Welcome to the White House, Mrs. Stowe." The lieutenant puffed up his chest as if he were announcing her visit to the world, but he gave Austin and Drew a cautious look.

"However, I must say the invitation was for you alone, not for you and…"

"These are our internaut guests, and they're coming in with me. I'm sure they would love to see President Lincoln." Never mind her size. Mrs. Stowe didn't seem at all afraid of the lieutenant. "Now, if you'll direct us to the Oval Office, please."

"Who is this lady?" Drew whispered to Austin as they followed another man down a long corridor.

"Harriet Beecher Stowe," Austin whispered back. He'd answered this question in a Knowledge Bowl contest once. "Famous novelist of the mid-1800s. She wrote *Uncle Tom's Cabin,* a story about what slavery really did to people. It blew readers away, sold hundreds of thousands of copies the first year it came out."

"Good book, huh? Maybe we should do our report on her instead, since we haven't been able to find C. S. Lewis."

"Yeah, maybe. Her book sure helped change history."

"Well, now," interrupted Mrs. Stowe, "I'm not sure I would say *that* exactly. I was only holding the pen."

She smiled and went on. "And now it's Mr. Lincoln who should be changing history. I believe he means well, but I'm not certain he understands the right thing to do about the slavery issue yet. He *must* sign the Emancipation Proclamation everyone is talking about."

The assistant who led them to the Oval Office must have heard her, since his eyebrows went up. But even if he was worried about letting troublemakers in to see the president of the United States, he still opened the door to the most famous office in the world.

"Mr. President," he barked, "Harriet Beecher Stowe of Hartford, Connecticut, and…er…two internauts."

If Mrs. Stowe was nervous about meeting Abraham Lincoln, she didn't show it. She marched right up to him and offered her hand. So she was going to set him straight about the evils of slavery, was she?

"So very glad to finally meet you, Mrs. Stowe." The president had to lean down to shake her hand, and he met her with a slow grin. A half-dozen staff and military men clustered around the room, some surrounded with cigar smoke. "So you are the little woman who wrote the book that made this big war."

They all chuckled, and she caught her breath, maybe not expecting that kind of remark from the president. But the serious look in his deep, dark eyes told everyone he meant it.

*The little woman who wrote the book that made this big war.*

That's what she had done with her words, hadn't she?

"And I see you brought your friends?" asked the president.

Austin wasn't sure what he was supposed to say to the sixteenth president of the United States, or even to the Web character playing him. "You were the greatest, Mr. Lincoln"? "They named an aircraft carrier after you, Mr. Lincoln"? "They put up a big statue of you here in Washington, D.C., and put your face on zillions of coins"?

Instead Austin managed to squeak, "Er…hi, sir."

He put out his sweaty hand just as a soldier burst in through the door.

"Everyone upstairs!" he yelled, and an outside window shattered as he spoke. Spam flooded in, spilling across the carpet and hitting the president before he could jump out of the way.

Outside a giant wave had already washed across the White House lawn in an unstoppable tide. There was nothing to do now but run for higher ground—if they could find some that was high enough.

But Austin didn't have time to find any. As he kicked through a mess of spam, everything went fuzzy.

# Bad to Worse

*No,* Ashley repeated to herself. *God is not done with us yet.* But she started thinking that Tucker could take what she had said two different ways. Either He had more for them to live for—which is what Ashley had meant—or He was going to let this storm send the Campbells' house into orbit.

Tucker wasn't saying what *she* thought. But for the next few moments, she squeezed the life out of Ashley's hand, and Ashley let her. Because, to tell the truth, Ashley was trembling too. And those moments of shaking and rattling and roaring were probably the longest of Ashley's life.

"I'm glad you're here, Ashley," whispered Tucker, still squeezing her hand.

"Me, too," Ashley whispered back. It didn't seem weird to say.

Jessi had her eyes closed, moving her lips as if she was praying. Mrs. Campbell sat on the other side of her daughter, saying things like "We'll be fine" and "It's going to be okay."

Well, during those moments when the twister was passing over them, it sure didn't sound as if everything was going to be okay. It sounded as if they were going to be sucked into the tornado any second.

But they weren't. Then all of a sudden it was very quiet, as if someone had turned off a power switch and the storm was all gone. Just like that. Unfortunately, the Campbells' power had blinked out too, so Mrs. Campbell snapped on her flashlight, adding to the flickering light of the battery-powered night-light.

Things had gone from a noise that had sounded like the end of the world to total silence, with nothing in between. Still, they huddled in their basement shelter. Ashley was sure no one wanted to be the first to move, but she knew she'd have to see what had happened upstairs. This time she couldn't just look away as she did when they showed accidents or disasters on the evening news.

No one said anything as they slowly got up and tiptoed up the stairs.

"It's still here!" Tucker was the first to break their silence. "The kitchen, the living room—everything!"

So far, so good. Ashley vaulted up the last three stairs and looked around for herself. True, the house still stood. But the moment they stepped into the front entry, Ashley knew something was wrong. She could feel a cool, damp draft moving through the house. Maybe a window had blown out.

They hurried down the main hall to the bedrooms, Tucker in the lead. But Tucker froze at the entrance to her room, and it wasn't hard to see why.

"Oh no," Jessi gasped and pushed aside a dripping oak branch, which was attached to the tree trunk that had crashed through the roof and taken out most of the outside wall. The tree had come to rest on the pile of stuffing and splinters that had once been Tucker's bed and desk.

No one else said anything in the weird stillness. Weirder yet, a ray of sunshine filtered in through the branches, as if the tornado had never been there. But the crushed remains of this part of the Campbells' house told them it *had* been there, at least for a few seconds.

Tucker buried her face in her hands and started crying once more. Ashley slipped an arm around her shoulders until Mrs. Campbell came over and gave her daughter a hug.

Suddenly Ashley thought of Austin…and his computer. She waded into the wreckage to check out the desk. Because if the laptop they had seen there really *had* been Austin's, his way home had been crushed just as surely as Tucker's room.

"Everybody okay in here?" A neighbor must have come in through the front door.

"We're all fine, thanks," answered Mrs. Campbell, wiping the dark traces of mascara from under her eyes.

The man stepped in to see for himself.

"We were lucky," he told them, but Ashley knew their safety had nothing to do with luck. "Everyone's houses are still standing. Looks like you and your next-door neighbor caught the worst of it, but at least you're all okay."

The man shook his head. "Weirdest thing I ever saw. That tornado reached down and then must have changed its mind and just skipped off. Nobody can ever predict those things."

Jessi joined them with a twisted piece of metal and electronics in her hand, looking as if she still wasn't sure what she'd discovered.

"My new laptop." Tucker accepted it from Jessi.

So it wasn't Austin's after all. Ashley sighed. That was both good news...and bad.

"That can be replaced," sighed Mrs. Campbell, her arms locked around her daughter. "All this can be replaced. I'm just thankful we're all okay."

They stood there for a few minutes, as if letting what had happened sink in.

"We need to contact your father," Mrs. Campbell said. "And these girls' parents as well."

*And tell them what?* Ashley bit her lip. *That Austin and Drew are missing on the Internet? And they have no way to get out?*

# CHAPTER 20

# Net Steaming

It took a minute for the fancy woven carpet of the Oval Office to change into a rough rope mat. Then another minute for Abraham Lincoln, who was sitting behind his presidential desk, to change into another bearded man in shorts sitting at a simple picnic table piled with papers, books, and a laptop. Two other men in worn shorts and T-shirts sat with him, their skin as dark as his was light. The man looked up when Austin and Drew arrived at...

Where were they?

Sunlight streamed through cracks in the bamboo wall and the single window that opened to a hillside below. The steamy heat felt so real that Austin almost forgot this wasn't the Outside.

"That was very odd," said the man, wiping his brow. "For a minute there I was almost sure I was sitting in the Oval Office of the White House."

"Uh…" Austin fanned himself and wondered how to explain.

"Well, maybe it was just a programming glitch." The man stood up. "We've been seeing quite a few of those lately. That and spam! But welcome!"

The man told Austin and Drew he was the Web version of Greg Henderson and that he'd been on *www.TranslatingThe Word.org* since March of 2000. "We've seen 3,479 hits this month—that's visits to you internauts—and now I'm working on a New Testament for the Arapesh people of Papua New Guinea."

A see-through map popped up next to his head, and a blinking star showed where they were on the map—a large island just north of Australia and south of the equator. That explained why Austin felt as though he'd walked into a steam bath.

"Today Mattias and Aluis here are working with me." He pointed to the other two men, who both smiled and nodded. Outside, the sun darkened and a drizzle began. "We're working on the book of Acts in their language. Click on Continue to find out how."

Drew hit the Continue button floating right in front of them before Austin could stop him.

"Actually," Austin tried to interrupt, "we're trying to find a way home. Hopefully a way that will take us around the spam storms."

Greg Henderson didn't seem to hear him.

"What we're doing is trying to find just the right words to make the Word of God come alive in a new language," he told them. *Poof!* Greg's wife appeared in the kitchen corner holding a loaf of bread. She didn't say anything, though, and Austin guessed maybe she wasn't programmed to talk.

Greg kept on with his guided tour.

"Take 'bread of life,' for instance, which is what Jesus called Himself in the Bible. Since we English speakers eat a lot of bread, we know exactly what that means. But what about some places in Mexico where they eat tortillas all the time? In those places when we translate the Bible, Jesus isn't the 'bread of life.' In some Mexican-Indian languages, we've translated John 6:35 and 6:48 so Jesus says, 'I am the tortilla of life.' Any questions so far? Click Yes or No."

Austin touched the glowing blue box in front of him that said Yes.

"We're looking for a way to try your e-mail," he said. "Do you think—"

"Ah yes. E-mail keeps us in touch with the home office and helps us do our job much more quickly. We keep it hooked into our shortwave radio. Other questions?"

Austin sighed.

"What about this link here?" Drew asked, pointing to *Outtakes* and *Bloopers*.

"Of course." Greg Henderson jumped right on that. "I knew you'd find that link sooner or later. We do our best not to make mistakes, but languages are very, very complicated. One time a missionary to the Tarahumara people was trying to learn how to say the word *jump,* so he acted it out. Wouldn't you do the same thing?"

Greg bounced up and down on the cabin floor while his two translator friends stared and laughed.

"What's the word for jump?" he asked. "Our missionary friend jotted down what the people told him. He didn't find out until later that he had written 'What's wrong with you?' in their language."

Drew laughed aloud as their host went on to another blooper.

"Or how about the missionary in West Africa who wanted to tell the Bible story about how the children of Israel crossed the Red Sea and followed Moses. Well, he almost got it right. But by making a very small mistake, he actually ended up writing 'The children of Israel crossed the red mosquitoes and swallowed Moses.' "

Greg finally stopped and sat on the corner of his table. His

wife disappeared—*poof!*—and so did his translator friends—
*poof, poof!*

He looked Austin straight in the eye. "You're not here for
the outtakes and bloopers, are you?"

Austin shook his head no. "We're just trying to get—"

Greg held up his hand. "Get home. I actually did hear
you. And I'm sorry...I don't know how to help."

"Not even a little?" Austin felt his heart sink.

"We're a long way out here, and my e-mail has been offline. I was actually hoping to keep you here a little longer by
doing my clueless Web-guide act. I'm sorry."

"Oh." Austin shrugged. "It's okay. I liked your stories.
They reminded me of another guy I met in Antwerp. He was
doing the same kind of thing as you. Only he—"

Austin didn't finish the story about how William Tyndale
had lived and died. As he fingered the New Testament in his
pocket, he figured Greg had probably already heard all about
it. Drew tapped on his shoulder as the rain outside turned to
a low, rumbling thunder.

"Another report from *Your Web Weather-dot-com*."

They turned to see the Web announcer once again; he'd
popped up in the open window of Greg's cabin, with the pouring rain for a backdrop. But this time he'd traded his cheery
smile for a worried frown.

"Chad Spaminelli here. We have confirmed reports now of serious spam storms globbing together into one giant flash flood, wiping out everything in its path." He rubbed his hands together as the nice sound of pouring rain in the background turned to a roar like that of Niagara Falls. "I was going to show you the map, but at this point it won't do you any good. If you're in its way...you're toast."

# CHAPTER 21

# Web-MaiLed

Austin remembered what it was like to be caught up in a big, breaking ocean wave. When he was ten, his family had driven all the way to Cocoa Beach, Florida, to visit their aunt Donna, and his dad had let him swim a short way out into the warm Atlantic Ocean. He'd thought it was great fun to ride the waves and topple into the sand—until he'd swallowed a mouthful of salt water.

This was far worse, and it wasn't water. He caught a breath here and there as they went through the spin cycle of junk e-mail. After the warning from Chad Spaminelli, they'd really had only about ten seconds before the wave hit. And Chad was right: This was nothing like the tame flood that had washed through the streets of digital Oxford, or even the flood that had followed them to Abraham Lincoln's virtual White House.

"Drew!" Austin tried to yell, but the spam seemed to swallow his voice, so he gave up. He thought he saw Drew a couple of times for a second or two, but he felt like a sock recognizing its mate in the washer before tumbling away.

Once more he was hit in the face with junk e-mail like the kind they'd heard before, only this time it was louder and worse.

"FREE!"

"SPECIAL OFFER!"

"ACT NOW!"

The phony deals, the schemes, the empty promises. He almost wished he were deaf. But the flood piled words on words and then mixed them together until Austin could hardly recognize them. He did see Drew whoosh by, and his friend managed to grab Austin's leg as they swirled around the World Wide Blender.

"My pants!" Austin yelled. "You're pulling my pants!"

Drew had clamped on to Austin's ankle and was holding on for the ride. Meanwhile, Austin wondered what was going on with the Tyndale New Testament in his pocket. It was vibrating like crazy—the way his dad's pager did when somebody needed him at the hospital.

*Weird.* But what happened next was even weirder.

Ashley picked her way through the fallen branches, almost expecting her own home to be crushed like Tucker's bedroom.

It wasn't.

"Careful of any wires, Ash." For once Jessi had no trouble keeping up. "We don't want to get electrocuted."

"I know." Ashley shuffled up the front walk, slowing with each step. She stopped halfway, next to a pile of blown-down branches, and turned to her aunt.

"But I don't know what I'm going to tell Mom and Dad."

"You'll think of something. You always do."

"But it's no good. No matter what I say, it's not going to bring Austin back."

"Maybe he figured out a way home. He's never been gone this long. Your brother always figures out a way."

"Then where is he? It's been a long time. He's stuck in there, and you know it, Jessi."

Jessi didn't answer. They both jumped when they heard a horn blaring behind them and wheels screeching to a stop at the curb in front of the Webster home.

"Ashley!" Her mom yelled, but her dad crossed the lawn first and scooped her close. And that's when the tears let loose.

"Oh, wow!" Austin stared at the ceiling in a little bedroom he'd never seen before. A *real* bedroom, not an Internet copy.

It was kind of messy, especially the bed and all the dirty

clothes stuffed underneath. But he liked the Chicago Cubs poster. And he had a feeling he knew who belonged to the scuffed skateboard propped up in the corner.

"That was amazing." Drew picked himself off the floor and handed Austin's shoe back to him—guess that one had been torn off in the flood. For the second time that day, Drew's clothes looked as if he'd just fallen into a swimming pool.

Next to them, on a crowded little desk, Austin's trusty silver laptop purred and sputtered.

"Crazy," agreed Austin. He checked the computer to make sure it was running okay. And he patted the Bible still in his pocket, knowing that Michael J. Tyndale hadn't given up on them. He must have kept trying Austin's e-mail address until it worked.

"Absolutely nuts," said Drew.

"Insane."

"Wigged out."

They both looked at each other and grinned.

"Don't say it"—Austin put up his hand—"because we are not going back in for a long, long time."

"Fine with me. I just want to know how we ended up in..." He looked up at the license-plate sign hanging by the door, and his jaw dropped.

*Nick's Room.*

They stood there, dripping wet, as they heard footsteps coming down the hallway.

"Nicholas!" A woman's voice called from downstairs. "You need to take that computer back to the school as soon as—"

"Yeah, Mom." Nick Ortiz tripped into his room and froze. He flapped his mouth, trying awfully hard to say something.

"Sorry to just bust into your room like this," Austin said at last.

"Yeah," added Drew. "We just thought we'd come by for the computer. Save you the trouble."

"Wait a minute. You don't think I…" Nick looked from his door to the computer and back. "I mean, I don't know how you got in here, but I didn't steal your laptop. I was cleaning trash cans after school, right? So the janitor opened the practice rooms, and I started to pick up some coats, and there it was—your laptop. After what you guys said about that Mr. Z, I just thought I should keep it safe for you. I tried to find you before the storm."

"You heard about the storm?" Drew asked.

"Heard about it? Where have you guys been?"

"Uh…" Austin was pretty sure they weren't going to be able to explain this one.

"Yeah," Nick went on. "I even told my mom. You can ask her if you want. I was just turning it on now to test it out. And I thought—"

"I believe you." Austin patted his computer and breathed easy for the first time all day. So his return ticket home had worked the way it should have after all.

"You do?" Nick swallowed hard. "No kidding?"

"Sure, we do," Drew joined in. "We believe you, okay?"

"But listen." Austin thought of something else. "Do you think I can use your phone for a sec? I have to call my sister."

He tucked the laptop under his arm and headed for the door.

"Oh, and one more thing," he added. "We should get together soon. Don't we have a report to write?"

# The Hyperlinkz Guide to Safe Surfing

Ashley Webster here. Are you seeing a pattern the way I am? Every time Austin lands in the Internet, look how lost he gets!

*Austin:* Wait a minute. If you're going to write the ending, you're going to have to be fair about this.

*Ashley:* I'm going to be fair, and I'm going to be honest. Wasn't it Margaret Thatcher who said that if you want anything said, ask a man. If you want anything done, ask a woman.

*Austin:* Hey, not fair!

*Ashley:* Are you going to let me have a turn at this or not? Austin tiptoed all over the Internet, but now it's my job to help you make some sense of it. So first let me tell you that in Illinois, where we live, we usually see about thirty tornadoes a year, and every single county in our state has had at least one since 1950. Tornadoes happen most often in April, May, and June. But one of the largest tornadoes ever struck on August 28, 1990. Tornadoes are serious stuff.

So was the life of William Tyndale, one of the bravest Bible translators ever—and one of the first. He really did have to run to Antwerp to get away from King Henry VIII, who thought having a Latin Bible was good enough and that William shouldn't mess with it. Never mind that hardly anyone could read Latin. Anyway, another Englishman, Henry Philips, betrayed Tyndale in the streets of Antwerp, very much the way it happened in our story. Tyndale was thrown into a dungeon and later executed for what he believed and did. You can find out all about the life of William Tyndale at—where else?— *www.williamtyndale.com*.

*Austin:* Do we need to say that some of the Web sites in this adventure are real and some of them aren't?

*Ashley:* We've said it before, but I guess we can tell people again. You won't be able to find some of the Web sites Austin and Drew visited, although some are based on real sites. Like if you want to find out all the famous people who went to Oxford University, there's a list at *www.damtp.cam.ac.uk/user/ smb1001/oxfalumn.htm*. That's actually a pretty ugly Web address, and there's no telling if it'll work when you try it. But you can always do a search for "Oxford alumni" (try using *www.google.com*), and you'll probably find it that way.

What's really cool is how Oxford was the school that so many different important people attended over hundreds of years. Like William Tyndale and Margaret Thatcher, who both went there. Margaret Thatcher was my favorite British prime minister ever, and you can find out all about her at *www.margaretthatcher.org.* Though I'm not sure if her family really did have an air-raid shelter, she really did eat canned meat during the war! And if you dig around the Web a little, you might even find a speech she once made about her Christian faith. She was a real fan of C. S. Lewis, one of my favorite writers.

Which reminds me, did you notice that Austin never got to meet Mr. Lewis, even after all his wandering around the Web? I think that proves my first point about the difference between boys and girls.

*Austin:* Here we go again.

*Ashley:* Okay, I'm sorry. I just couldn't help slipping that in. And I just can't help slipping in a plug for one of the coolest sites I've seen in a long time: *www.wycliffe.org.* The kids' section is especially fun with stories and puzzles and stuff. You can get there from the Wycliffe home page or zip there directly by keying *www.wycliffe.org/kids.* Either way, it's all about people who have spent their lives translating the Bible into different languages for those who don't have it.

*Austin:* Yeah, and did you know that there are still 250 million people in the world who don't have a single Scripture verse in their language? And did you know that there are about 6,800 languages in the world, but more than 3,000 of them don't have any of the Bible? Only 405 languages have a whole Bible—both the Old and New Testaments.

*Ashley:* That's the Chiddix Knowledge Bowl champion for you, just getting warmed up.

*Austin:* Maybe all those big numbers don't mean much by themselves. Look at it this way: Pretend you had a model of the world, and it had only one hundred people in it. From what I said about people and Bibles, that means only six of those one hundred people would have a complete Bible, Genesis to Revelation, in their own language! On the other hand, forty-four of those one hundred people would have no Bible at all. The rest would just have bits and pieces.

*Ashley:* Here's the thing: Translators like Tyndale have to work hard so people can have the Word of God in their own language. And then there are other people who work with words in a totally different way—people like Harriet Beecher Stowe, who put words together in stories that made people think. She had to work hard too. And though we're not totally sure what American president Abraham Lincoln said when he met her, look what her words did!

*Austin:* On the other hand, there's a lot of junk washing around out there—spam, for one (the e-mail kind, not the meat kind). I know all about how important it is to stay away from it. Ah, is that about all you had to say, Ashley?

*Ashley:* One more thing. If you don't already know it, there really is a Chiddix Junior High in Normal, Illinois. It's a great school in a great town. But even though we borrowed the school name for the story, the real school is different. For one thing, we've changed the names of the teachers and the principal. And besides, the *real* Chiddix Junior High principal would never hire a sub as weird as Mr. Z!

See ya,

Ashley (and Austin)


P.S. to parents: The Internet can be a lot of fun. But please make sure your child is surfing safely. That means being there for them. Know what they're accessing. And *please* consider a good filtering service or software, since it can help you sidestep some nasty surprises. We can't tell you to use one service over another, but you might start by checking out a great site called *www.filterreview.com*. It'll give you all the choices.

Please visit Robert Elmer's Web site at *www.RobertElmerBooks.com* to learn more about other books he's written or to schedule him to speak to your school or home-school group.